PAPERCUTZ™

#2 GORILLA VS BEAR

SLAIUM / MENG — Story
BLACK INK TEAM — Art
BLACK INK TEAM — Cover Illustration
SENG YAO / SANTA FUNG / PUPPETEER — Illustrators
KC / SIEW — Coloring
KIAT — Translator

KENNY CHUA — Creative Director
KIAONG — Art Director
BEAN — Original Graphic & Layout
NIUH JIT ENG / ROSS BAUER — Original Editors

MARK McNABB — Editor & Production
JEFF WHITMAN — Managing Editor
INGRID RIOS — Editorial Intern
JIM SALICRUP
Editor-in-Chief

Papercutz books may be purchased for business or promotional use.
For information on bulk purchase please contact Macmillan
Corporate and Premium Sales Department at (800) 221-7945 x5442.

ISBN HC: 978-1-5458-0626-5
ISBN PB: 978-1-5458-0627-2

Printed in China.
February 2021

Distributed by Macmillan
First Papercutz Printing

X-VENTURE XPLORERS™
KINGDOM OF ANIMALS

#2 GORILLA VS BEAR

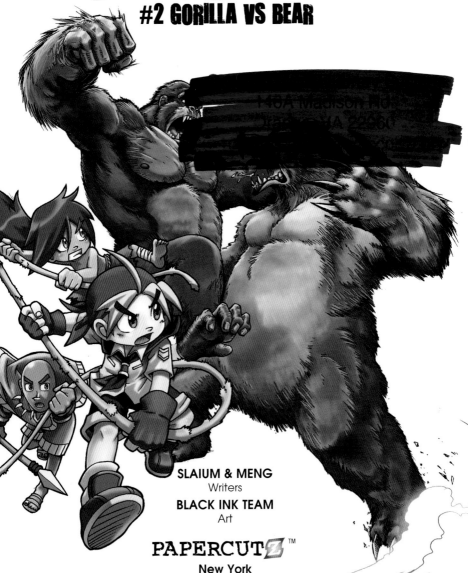

SLAIUM & MENG
Writers

BLACK INK TEAM
Art

PAPERCUTZ™
New York

FOREWORD

As a result of the publication of numerous educational comics in recent years, the perception of comics as frivolous and fantastical fiction has slowly been changed. For students, the partnership of words and pictures has been observed to enhance information retention, and consequently comics are having an increasingly important role as part of the learning process. Educational comics have become one of the sources of extra-curricular knowledge; harnessing young learner's enthusiasm for well-visualized and creative stories which simultaneously convey comprehensible information.

X-VENTURE XPLORERS pits animal antagonists against each other. Battles between beasts of similar strength such as Lion Vs. Tiger, Elephant Vs. Rhinoceros, Boa Vs. Crocodile and so forth not only offer young learners the joy of reading, but also a starting point to enjoy learning about the natural world.

Upholding the principle of interesting scientific knowledge central to any X-VENTURE XPLORERS comic series, we provide young minds the space for imagination and help them explore the wonders of natural science. As an educational comic, this series prioritizes the moral values of love and friendship, courage and the joy of learning so as to help nurture the right values in our readers.

Incisive information alongside vivid visuals, interspersing the chapters of the story provide readers with ample and accessible knowledge of wildlife and their world. Additionally, to gauge what they have learned, one can test their wits by answering a short quiz on what they have read. With equal emphasis on entertainment and education, it ought to be clear that X-VENTURE XPLORERS represents value, fun, and furnishes a fecund factual future for our formative friends!

CAST

SHERRY

Hardworking and a keen learner, she wishes to become a veterinarian. She assumes the role of peacemaker, especially between Jake and Louis who argue constantly.

JAKE

Brave and passionate, he enjoys the company of animals and is proud of being a boy scout. He is often careless, however, causing trouble for himself and his friends.

TAZEN

A little native with a huge appetite who grew up in the Sumatran rainforest, raised by orangutans. Has the ability to communicate with animals, but finds humans a harder prospect.

NLIZR

(Natural Life Zoographic Resource, more commonly known as "the analyzer") Dr. Darwin's e-evolution in evidence; able to record, analyze, extrapolate details pertaining to localized ecology, climate, lifeform identification, and much more via an instant uplink to the lab database.

LOUIS

Despite being loud, lazy, and constantly antagonizing Jake, he never accepts failure and is a very reliable partner during a crisis.

KWAME

A member of the Bushmen tribe of South Africa, he knows the wild like the back of his hand, constantly on the alert for potential threats, both animal and otherwise.

BEAN

Shy and quiet, and short in stature, makes up in extraordinary wealth of knowledge what he lacks in physical size.

DR. DARWIN

A renowned authority in the fields of biology and zoology, who remains in impeccable physical shape, despite his age, with a flair for the dramatic. Harsh but generous, he demands focus and discipline from the X-Venture team at all times, or else!

SMITH

Dr. Darwin's faithful assistant's dedicated diligence to his duties does him no favors when facing the ripping rages of his buff boss!

CONTENTS

CHAPTER 1 **FINDING TAZEN** 009
CHAPTER 2 **GORILLAS IN AMERICA!** 029
CHAPTER 3 **THE MYSTERIOUS METAL HEAD** 047
CHAPTER 4 **MAD DOC IN THE HOUSE** 065
CHAPTER 5 **MONKEY MAYHEM!** 083
CHAPTER 6 **ICE TO MEET YOU** 101
CHAPTER 7 **SCRATCH YOU LATER** 119
CHAPTER 8 **THE ULTIMATE SACRIFICE** 137

*Some animal sizes have been altered to make the comics as visually dramatic and exciting as possible

CHAPTER 1
FINDING TAZEN

TAKE CARE, **TAZEN,** ENJOY YOUR TRIP BACK HOME!
HERE! TAKE MY SPEAR WITH YOU FOR PROTECTION.

I CANNOT WAIT... TO REACH HOME... SEE MY FAMILY...

HUH?! WHAT'S THIS?!

WUU AAH?!
<MOM! WHAT HAPPENED?!>

NGAH BWA?
<WHERE'S DAD?>

BWA GRUH!
<DAD, I'M BACK!>

WOOK!
GRAH!

UUH-UH AAH!
YEEEEK!
All running away... why?
DAD!

GRRAWWH!!

GRRRRRL!

BWAK! NYEK! WUHAA?
<WHERE DID THIS BEAR COME FROM? IT'S HUGE!>

ARBWA? GRAK MUH?
SUN BEAR? YOU TOO? WHY ARE YOU ATTACKING MY FAMILY?!>

GROWL!

ERR, WHA?! <THEY DON'T SEEM TO UNDERSTAND ME...>

OHH! OOH! OOH!
GN UH BWAH! NURF! <DON'T WORRY, DAD. WE'LL BE OKAY.>

WARRH! <FOR MY FAMILY!>

RUH! <FOR MY MOM!>
EEEYAGH!

CHIII!

GRRRROWL...

SNAP

UUUUH...
DAD!

EEERK!

WRAAH!
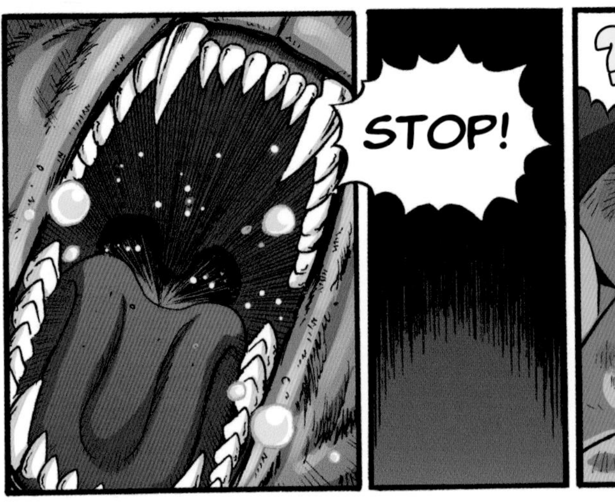
STOP!

?!

WHY IF IT ISN'T OUR TALKS-TO-CRITTERS FRIEND!

RIGHT YOU ARE, **BASH**! THE DOC WILL LIKE HIM!

3 DAYS LATER
GUYS!
IT'S BEEN OVER A WEEK AND TAZEN ISN'T BACK YET!

DO YOU THINK SOMETHING HAPPENED TO HIM?

RELAX! I'M SURE HE'S FINE. GIVE HIM A COUPLE MORE DAYS.

JAKE'S RIGHT, MY DEAR SHERRY, DON'T WORRY.

IF I MAY ASK, WHO IS TAZEN?

TAZEN IS OUR NEW TEAM MEMBER WHO WAS RAISED BY ORANGUTANS. SHERRY AND JAKE BROUGHT HIM HERE FROM SUMATRA, REMEMBER?

OH, UH! SORRY, MUST HAVE SLIPPED MY MIND...
SHEESH! ABSENT-MINDED GORILLA!

WHO ARE YOU CALLING A GORILLA, MONKEY BOY?!
YOU! THAT'S WHO!

STOP ARGUING RIGHT NOW!
OR ELSE...

Sorry Jake.
My bad, my bad.
UMMM, SIR, WE'RE RUNNING OUT OF WHITE COATS.

?!
SHOULDN'T WE FIND OUT WHAT HAPPENED?

HEY, GUYS, LOOKS LIKE TAZEN'S IN TROUBLE! COME TAKE A LOOK!

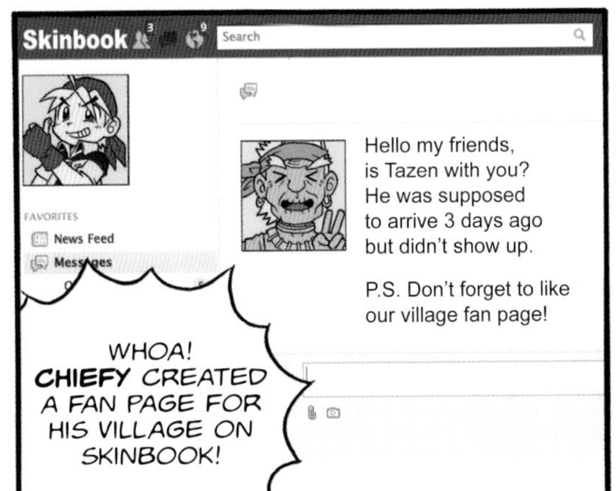
Skinbook
Search
FAVORITES
News Feed
Messages
Hello my friends, is Tazen with you? He was supposed to arrive 3 days ago but didn't show up.
P.S. Don't forget to like our village fan page!
WHOA! **CHIEFY** CREATED A FAN PAGE FOR HIS VILLAGE ON SKINBOOK!

HMM... IF THAT'S THE CASE, YOU GUYS BETTER GO TO SUMATRA AND INVESTIGATE.
I'LL MAKE THE NECESSARY ARRANGE-MENTS.

NO TIME TO WASTE! C'MON, SHERRY, LET'S GO!
HEY, WE CAN WAIT A FEW MORE DAYS. HE'S PROBABLY MONKEYING AROUND TOO MUCH!

LOUIS, TAZEN MAY BE IN TROUBLE!
HOW CAN YOU JUST SIT THERE? HE MAY NEED OUR HELP!

HE CAN LOOK AFTER HIMSELF...

LOUIS, PLEASE HELP US FIND TAZEN. DO IT FOR ME?

YEAH!
C'MON!

OKAY, COUNT ME IN... ANYTHING FOR YOU, SHERRY.

LET'S GO!
HEY? DON'T WE HAVE ANY LINES?

SUMATRA, INDONESIA.

APPARENTLY, SOMETHING BAD HAPPENED IN THE JUNGLE. THE ORANGUTANS WERE ATTACKED AND WE COULDN'T FIND TAZEN OR HIS DAD.

TAZEN'S MOM WAS BADLY INJURED BUT IS RECOVERING.

DON'T WORRY, **MRS. ORANG**. WE'LL FIND THEM!

EEEK!
NICE ORANG!

WE'LL LOOK AFTER HER, TILL YOU FIND TAZEN.

...AND FIND HIM WE WILL! NOW, SHOW US WHERE IT HAPPENED!
WHOA! JAKE IS SO PUMPED UP!

Guys, I found Tazen's sack...

HOW COULD MY SPECIALLY MADE SPEAR BREAK SO EASILY? WHAT COULD HAVE DONE THIS?
RIIIIIING...

JAKE, IT'S **DR. DARWIN!**

DOC, WASSUP? WE'RE AT THE SCENE OF THE CRIME!
JAKE, WE'VE JUST RECEIVED NEW INFORMATION...
ANIMALS NOT NATIVE TO NORTH AMERICA HAVE BEEN SIGHTED IN YELLOWSTONE NATIONAL PARK!

IT MIGHT BE RELATED TO TAZEN'S DISAPPEARANCE!
THIS TAKES PRIORITY! WE HAVE A PLANE EN ROUTE.
WE NEED TO REGROUP!

CLICK
OKAY...
THUMP
GAH!
HOW CAN WE LEAVE WITHOUT FINDING, TAZEN?!

WE CAN'T ABANDON HIM! HE'S OUR FRIEND!

BUT WE HAVE TO GO BACK TO BASE AS INSTRUCTED.
I'M TORN... WHAT SHOULD WE DO?

LOUIS! DON'T JUST STAND THERE! HELP US OUT HERE!

HMMM... KNOWING HIM, HE JUST WANTS TO GO HOME.

DAD? CAN YOU SEND YOUR PRIVATE JET TO SUMATRA? WE'RE HEADING TO AMERICA!
What?!

What is a bear?

Modern bears consist of eight species spread across North & South America, Europe, Asia and the North Pole. Despite their large size, most bears can move swiftly and are capable climbers and swimmers. They are largely omnivorous and eat a combination of meat and plants, except for the polar bear which is strictly carnivorous. The panda meanwhile is mostly herbivorous, with 99% of its diet consisting of bamboo shoots.

BROWN BEAR ANATOMY

Body

Bulky, sturdy, heavy bodies covered in thick fur and insulating fat.

Ears

Despite having small ears, the bear's hearing could be better than ours, probably in the ultrasonic range.

Eyes

Bears have color-vision but are myopic or near-sighted. This makes it difficult for them to distinguish objects at a distance, but is ideal for foraging close to the ground.

Limbs

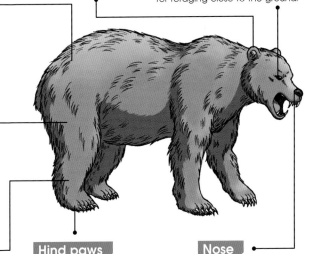

Although its limbs are thick and short, it can run quite fast, at over 31 miles per hour. Brown bears are not so adept at climbing trees due to their blunt claws.

Hind limbs

Although it can stand up and sit down like humans do, its weight tends to preclude walking on two feet.

Hind paws

Sturdy, powerfully muscled back limbs allow bears to rear up onto their hind limbs to reach food, and ward off attackers.

Nose

With a very keen sense of smell, a bear can detect the scent of a carcass nearly 3 miles away.

Teeth

The incisors and canine teeth are quite large while the molars are underdeveloped and usually lost at an early age.

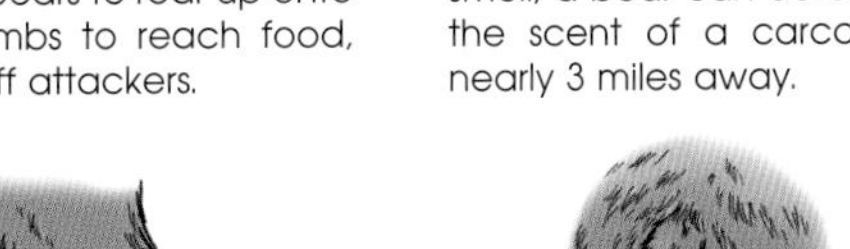

Front paws

Equipped with five non retractable claws, a bear's forepaws are used for climbing, slashing rivals, attackers, and prey or even hooking fish.

Tail

Measuring around 4.8 inches, it has no significant use.

Do bears hibernate?

Basically bears go into an inactive phase during winter called "hibernation." During this time, they can remain dormant for months without eating, drinking, and excreting waste, surviving only on their body fat. What differentiates bears from other true hibernating animals is that their body temperature does not drop substantially and they are easily awakened when winter ends. Some female bears even give birth, just before emerging from their winter sleep.

What do you do when you run into a bear?

Most bears avoid conflict and casualties caused by bear attacks are rare but not uncommon. If you encounter one, do NOT run. Back away or walk around the bear if possible. Use pepper spray if you have any but only as a defense. If an attack is imminent, drop onto your stomach or curl up in a fetal position, covering the back of your neck with your hands. Alternatively, make as much noise as you can and swing your arms waving a stick/rock to tell the bear you are not easy prey.

Human-Bear conflict

Conflicts between bears and humans are on the rise due to rapid urbanization in places such as North America and Asia. This loss of habitat causes bears to enter populated areas in search of food which invariably leads to them being killed when they become too aggressive toward humans. Meanwhile, across East and Southeast Asia, black bears are illegally captured and kept in bear farms for their bile. This inhumane practice causes them to suffer extreme physical and psychological pain.

PRIMATES

Vhat is a primate?

rimates are some of the most intelligent mammals on Earth compared to most other pecies in the animal kingdom. This could be attributed to their having a larger brain ompared to the rest.

PRIMATE CATEGORIZATION

Ring-tailed Lemur ▶

trepsirrhini

Comprises lemurs, pottos, lorises, and alagos. These primates are defined by neir wet noses, smaller brains, bigger lfactory lobes, and a reflective layer n their eyes for better night vision.

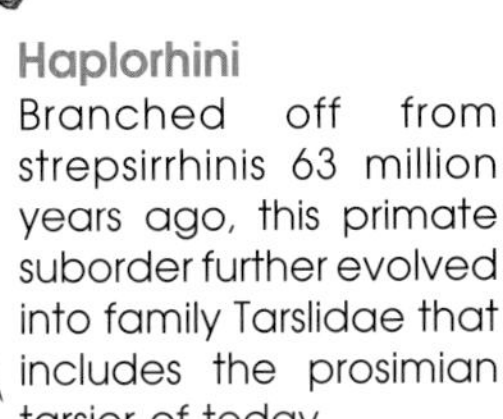

◀ Tarsier

Haplorhini

Branched off from strepsirrhinis 63 million years ago, this primate suborder further evolved into family Tarslidae that includes the prosimian tarsier of today.

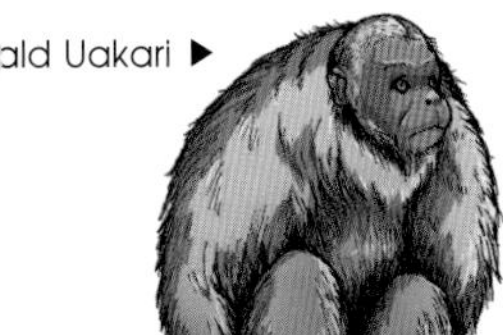

ald Uakari ▶

Simiiformes

The primates in this suborder are divided into two groups: - the flat-nosed or New World monkeys (Prehensile tails; capuchins, howlers) and narrow-nosed or Old World monkeys (baboons, macaques).

◀ Olive Baboon

New World monkeys		Old World monkeys
Central America and South America	**Distribution**	Asia and Africa
Small to medium	**Body size**	Medium to large
Flat and wide with nostrils facing sideways	**Nose**	Narrow with nostrils facing down
Prehensile, used as a fifth hand	**Tail**	Not used to grab Some lack tails
Mostly arboreal (tree-dwellers)	**Habitat**	Both terrestrial (on land) and arboreal

ape

Apes, members of super-family Hominoidea are native to Africa and Southeast Asia. As the largest tailless primates, ney are divided into two families – Hylobatidae (lesser apes - ibbons and siamang) and Hominidae (great apes – gorillas, rangutans, chimpanzee, bonobos, and humans).

Chimpanzee ▶

▼ Similar to other primates that are good at climbing trees, the common squirrel monkey is able to bend its fingers and toes like hooks to provide a firm grip.

Movement

Most primates have nimble limbs. For example, the gibbon uses its hands to swing from trees while lemurs jump from one tree to another. Apes like gorillas and chimpanzees move around by walking on all fours (knuckle-walking) and are capable of limited ambulation on two feet.

Tool users

Primates are very intelligent. They are able to hold objects with their hands — a trait that allows them to use tools. The picture on the left shows a capuchin trying to crack open a coconut using stones, while chimpanzees can use a stick to remove ants from its formicary or ant nest.

Social animals

The size and structure of all primate groups differ from one species to the other, and each has its own way of communicating. Members in the same group mostly partake of communal grooming, protection against enemies, and caring for the young. Internal conflicts do arise at times, especially when food is scarce or during mating.

CHAPTER 2
GORILLAS IN AMERICA?

The more we get together, together, together...

...the more we get together, the happier we'll be.

WOOOAAH!
DISH--
AAAAAH!
SHAA... VOOOH

YELLOWSTONE NATIONAL PARK, ESTABLISHED IN 1872, IS LOCATED PRIMARILY IN WYOMING AND IS WIDELY REGARDED AS THE FIRST NATIONAL PARK IN THE WORLD. IT'S KNOWN FOR ITS WILDLIFE AND MANY GEOTHERMAL FEATURES SUCH AS HOT SPRINGS AND GEYSERS. IT ALSO HAS MANY ECOSYSTEMS FROM THE SUBALPINE FOREST, TO GRASSLANDS, LAKES, CANYONS, RIVERS, AND MOUNTAIN RANGES.
MORE IMPORTANTLY, IT IS HOME TO HUNDREDS OF SPECIES OF MAMMALS, BIRDS, FISH, REPTILES, AND UNIQUE PLANT SPECIES...

...AND SPANS AN AREA OF 3,470 SQUARE MILES.
WOW! THAT'S HUGE!

SO, WHERE DO WE EVEN START LOOKING FOR TAZEN?!

HMMM! AND YOU CALL YOURSELF A BOY SCOUT!

FIRST RULE: ALWAYS SECURE A VANTAGE POINT TO GET A BETTER VIEW OF YOUR SURROUNDINGS.

SCOUTING 101 AND YOU CAN'T EVEN FIGURE THAT OUT?
YEAH, YEAH... WHATEVER!

JAKE! STOP TAKING PHOTOS. NOW'S NOT THE TIME!
HEHE... SERVES YOU RIGHT!

SOMETHING DOESN'T FEEL RIGHT...
WUU HUU
WUU HUU

GUYS, I NEED SOME HELP HERE.

CHIMPANZEES? IN AMERICA?! THEY'RE ONLY FOUND IN AFRICA!

THEY'RE SO CUTE! THEY MUST BE LOST.
ALL THE WAY FROM AFRICA TO AMERICA? THAT'S RIDICULOUS!

WELL... ANYWAY, THEY'RE TAME, SO--

NGAP AAAAAAA...

BEEEEEEEAN!

WUU WUU AHHAHH
SQUEAL

I'LL HOLD THEM BACK. YOU GUYS RUN!
BEAN! YOUR H-HAND!

N-NO, I'M OKAY!

KDAK

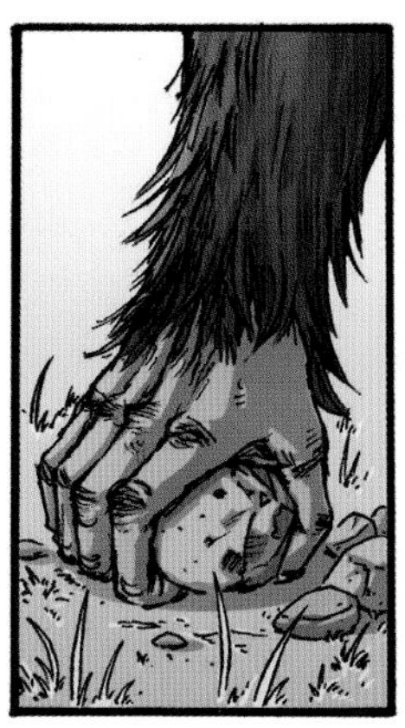

HEEEEELP!

UH?

LOUIS?!

CHIMPS ARE HIGHLY INTELLIGENT. THEY USE TOOLS AS WEAPONS OR TO HUNT!

EEEEEEK!

CHOMP

EAT TRANQUILIZER, CAESAR!

THERE ARE TOO MANY, I CAN'T TRANQ THEM ALL WITH ONE GUN!
WHAT'S GOING ON? THESE CHIMPS ARE TOO AGGRESSIVE, EVEN THE WILD ONES AREN'T THIS VIOLENT!

GRAAAH!

SHIIING
SHIIING

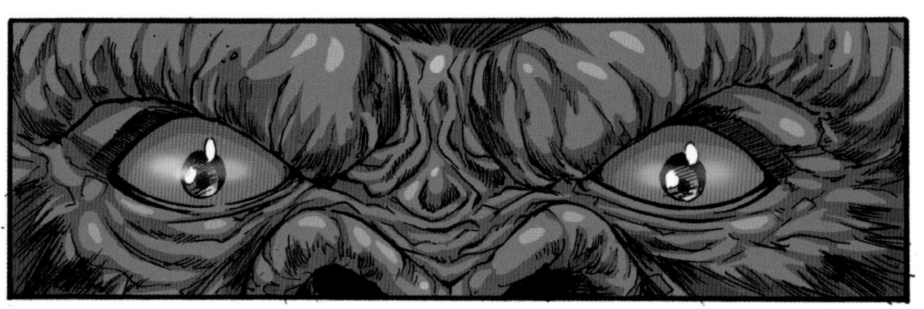

GRRRRRR!
OH... MY... GAWD! THAT IS THE BIGGEST CHIMPANZEE I'VE EVER SEEN!

THAT'S IT.
WE'RE DEAD...

WUU AAHH!

SWAT
UUUUH!

BEHOLD THE POWER OF THE SILVERBACK GORILLA!

JAKE, GO... GO TALK TO IT!
WHY ME? I'M NO TAZEN!

I'm afraid it'll grab me and climb up a tall building!
Oh, come on!

ERR... HELLO, **MR. KONG**. THANK YOU FOR... SAVING US FROM THOSE CHIMPS!

UMM!

LOOKS LIKE JAKE'S TRYING TO REMOVE THOSE CUFFS!

CLANG
CLANG

GLAD WE COULD HELP YOU IN RETURN BIG FELLA!

WOOSH...
WOOSH...

UUMM...

H-HEY, N-NO! OOF!

I THINK WE SHOULD HIDE!
YES! THE GORILLA SENSES TROUBLE...

GROWL!

THERE'S THE STUPID APE. AT LEAST IT DIDN'T GET TOO FAR!

※THE SAME POACHERS WE MET IN **X-VENTURE XPLORERS #1!**

GROWR
GROWL

SWIPE

KRAK

KRAK
POK

SHIIING
SLASH
SHIIING

CHUUUNG

THE BLACK BEAR'S CLAWS ARE CAUGHT. NOW IS THE CHANCE FOR THE GORILLA TO STRIKE!

PAAP

DROP KICK!
K.O.
GROOOH!
Woohooo... way to go, Kong!
BANG

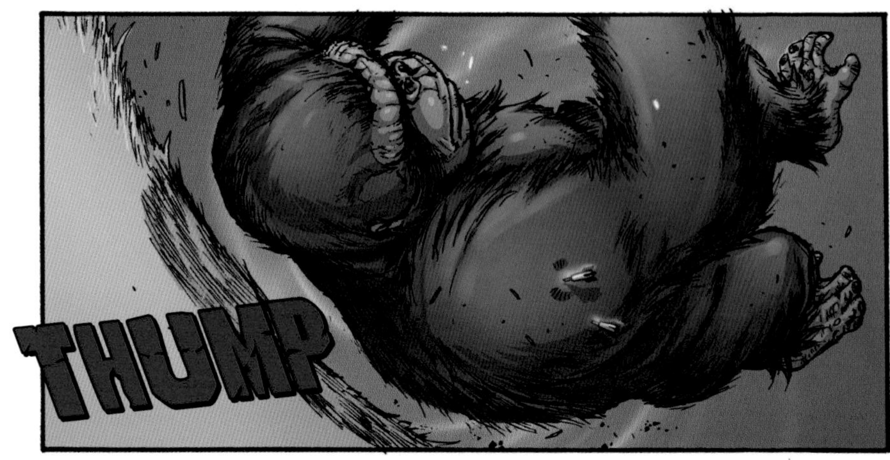
THUMP

KONG!

THAT'S ENOUGH! THE TRANQUILIZER SHOULD DO THE TRICK!

RIGHT, LET'S BAG EM!

Conservation Status

Extinct EX	Extinct in the Wild EW	Critically Endangered CR	Endangered EN	Vulnerable VU	Near Threatened NT	Least Concern LC

Species: Ursus americanus
Length (including tail): 4 to 6.8 feet
Weight: 90 to 660 pounds
Diet: Fruits, salmon, small vertebrates
Distribution: North America
Habitats: Forested areas

AMERICAN BLACK BEAR

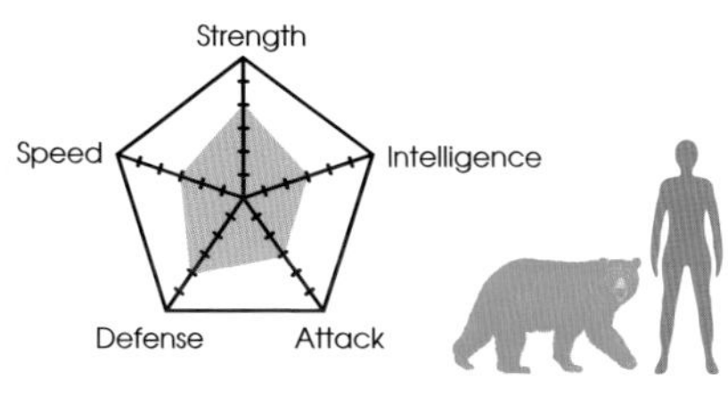

Despite its large size, the American black bear is not an apex predator. Its diet consists mostly of plants, fish, and the occasional smaller prey or carrion. They usually avoid confrontation with other predators such as wolves, and often climb trees when in danger. Since these bears eat dead animals, playing dead to avoid their attacks is not a good idea!

SUN BEAR

Conservation Status

Extinct EX	Extinct in the Wild EW	Critically Endangered CR	Endangered EN	Vulnerable VU	Near Threatened NT	Least Concern LC

Species: Helarctos malayanus
Length (including tail): 4 to 5 feet
Weight: 60 to 143 pounds
Diet: Fruits, insects, honey
Distribution: Southeast Asia and South Asia
Habitats: Tropical rainforest

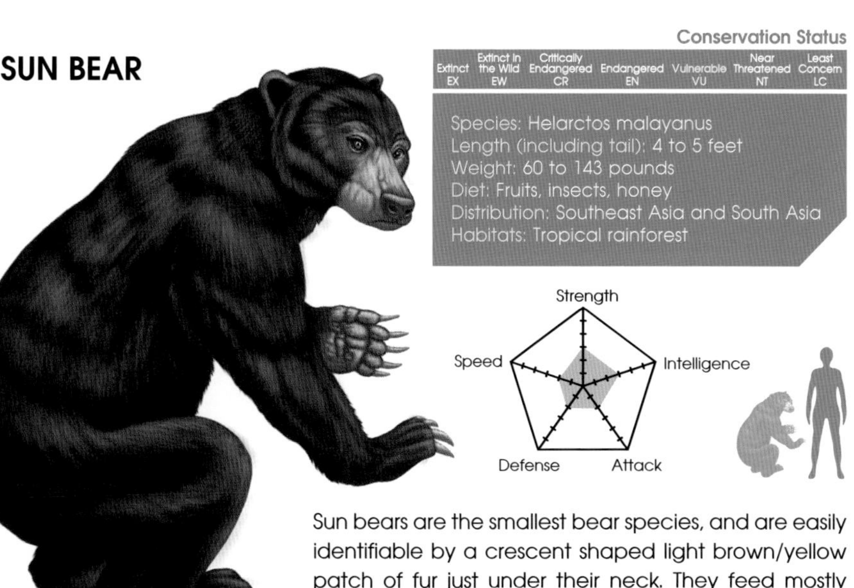

Sun bears are the smallest bear species, and are easily identifiable by a crescent shaped light brown/yellow patch of fur just under their neck. They feed mostly on honey, termites, and insects, using their long sickle-shaped claws to rip open tree bark or bee hives.

COMMON CHIMPANZEE

Conservation Status

Extinct EX	Extinct in the Wild EW	Critically Endangered CR	Endangered EN	Vulnerable VU	Near Threatened NT	Least Concern LC

Species: Pan troglodytes
Length: Up to 5.6 feet
Weight: 70 to 154 pounds
Diet: From fruit to medium-sized mammals
Distribution: Northwestern and Central Africa
Habitat: Grasslands to mountainous forests.

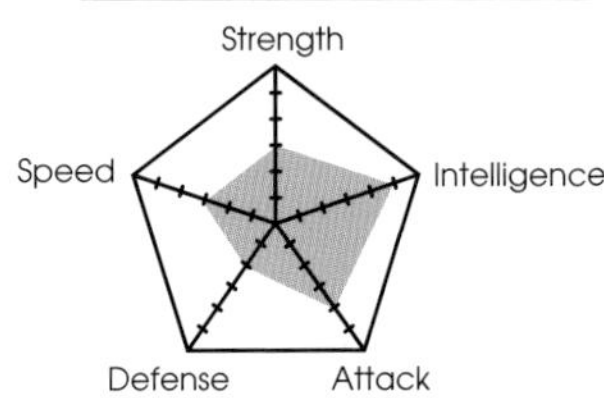

In taxonomy, chimpanzees are very similar to humans in their genetic make-up, with up to almost a 98% genetic match. They can walk upright, use tools, and spend their time both on the ground and in trees. With an intelligence level equivalent to that of a five to seven year old child, chimps are one of the smartest animals in the world. They are highly emotional and social creatures, and some have even been taught to use sign language to communicate with humans.

BONOBO

Conservation Status

Extinct EX	Extinct in the Wild EW	Critically Endangered CR	Endangered EN	Vulnerable VU	Near Threatened NT	Least Concern LC

Species: Pan paniscus
Length: Up to 3.8 feet
Weight: 66 to 132 pounds
Diet: From fruit to insects and small mammals
Distribution: Central Africa
Habitat: Forests

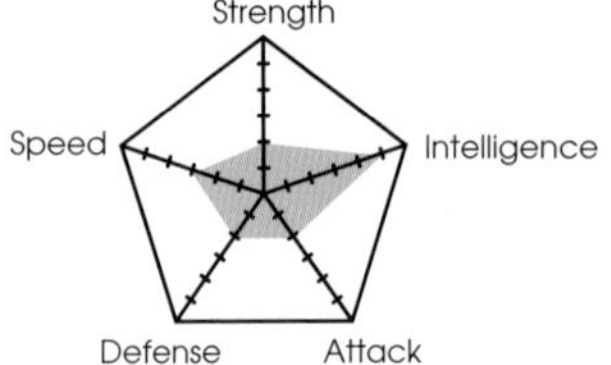

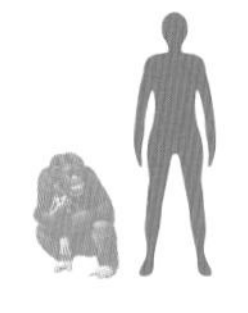

Bonobos resemble their close cousins, chimpanzees, but have longer limbs, less fur, and smaller heads. Female bonobos tend to have a higher status and, in general, these gracile chimpanzees, as bonobos are sometimes called, are more peaceful and sociable compared to chimps.

CHAPTER 3

THE MYSTERIOUS METAL HEAD

FOLLOW THE CHOPPER! IT MIGHT BRING US TO TAZEN!
UUUUH! WHAT THE--?

THIS IS SCI-FI TERRITORY! A METAL HEAD IN THE MIDDLE OF NOWHERE!

LOOK! THERE'S A DOOR. THAT'S OUR TICKET IN!
YOU BUFFOON! WE'LL BE CAUGHT FOR SURE USING THE MAIN ENTRANCE! WE NEED ANOTHER WAY IN.

FOUND IT... OVER HERE, GUYS!

DANG! THIS PLACE STINKS!

YAKKK... THE STENCH IS UNBEARABLE...
JAKE! YOU BETTER GET US OUT OF HERE FAST!
STOP MOANING, GUYS, C'MON MOVE IT!

I THINK THIS IS WHERE THEY KEEP THE CAPTURED PRIMATES!
No wonder...

...THIS PLACE REALLY SMELLS BAD!

LET ME SEE WHAT'S UP TOP...

I THINK WE'RE RIGHT IN THE...
UM, HEH!
PLOP

NICE GOING, BOY BLUNDER! BRINGING US IN VIA THE SEWER!
HAHA! GIVE IT TO HIM, SHERRY!

HMM...

WOW! THERE'S A BAMBOO FOREST IN HERE!

SHH! DON'T STARTLE THE PANDAS...

SO, YOU'RE ALL KISS* FANS?

SWAT
GROWL!

What on Earth were you thinking, Jake?

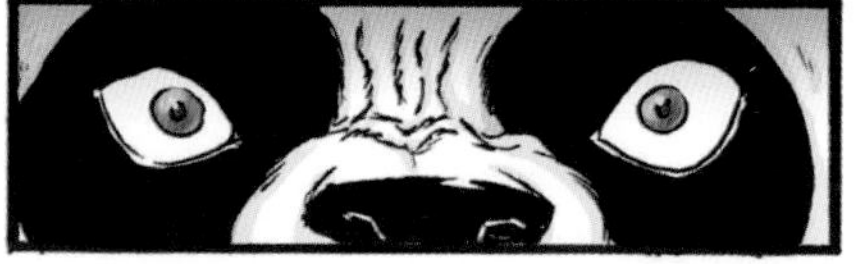

AREN'T PANDAS PEACEFUL? WHY ARE THEY ATTACKING US?!

THE PANDAS USED TO BE CARNIVOROUS A LONG TIME AGO. PERHAPS THEY STILL HAVE AGGRESSIVE GENES IN THEM?

LOUIS, DON'T CLIMB UP, IT'LL BREAK!

NOT VERY FUNNY!

※ KISS: AN AMERICAN ROCK BAND FAMOUS FOR THE BAND MEMBERS' BLACK AND WHITE FACE PAINT.

GREAT, SEE WHAT YOU'VE DONE? IT'S BENDING ALL THE WAY TO THE GROUND!

LOUIS!

GRAA!

WMPF

GRRR...

HUH? I KNOCKED IT OUT COLD!
WHIMPER...

YEE-HAW! I DID IT! I SAVED THE DAY. I'M THE HERO!

TWOOING
YOU GUYS CAN COME DOWN... NOW!?
!

UUH, NICE PLAN, LOUIS. A WARNING WOULD HAVE HELPED.

NYEH?!

KONG!

HE'S OKAY!

HEY, BIG GUY, WE'RE HERE TO SAVE YOU!

Hehehe...
ABOUT TIME YOU KIDS GOT HERE!

CWONG
CWONG
CWONG
!!
DANG! THEY FOUND US!

C'MON, C'MON... GOTTA PICK THIS LOCK FAST!

GROWR!
GROWR!

YIKES! A PACK OF CRAZY SLOTH BEARS!

GWAR!

GRRRRR!

GROWL!

GRRRRR!

SLOTH BEARS HAVE VERY POWERFUL PAWS WITH EXTREMELY SHARP CLAWS. BE CAREFUL, GUYS!

SHIIING

GROOOH!
HOLD ON, BIG FELLA, I'M ALMOST DONE.

AT LAST!

WAARH!

CHOMP
WHACK

THERE ARE TOO MANY BEARS! LET ME HELP YOU OUT!
HEE YAAAH!

KRAK

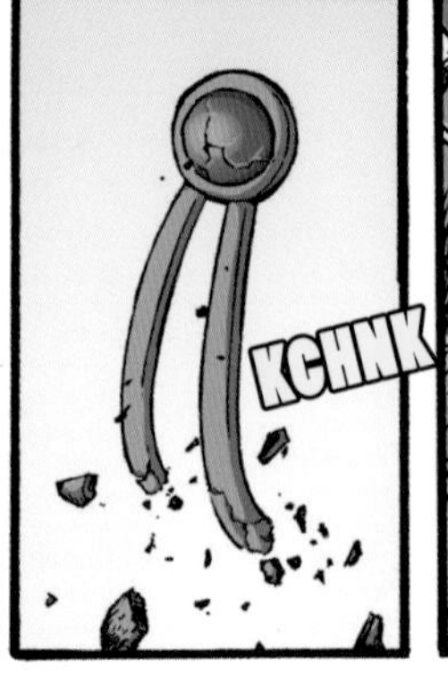
KCHNK

GGRRR URRR?

SMAK

THE BEARS ARE CONTROLLED BY THE HEADSETS! WE MUST DESTROY THE HEADSETS!

Nice one!
GROWL

KLUNK

SPOOSH

SLOTH BEARS HAVE A KEEN SENSE OF SMELL BUT POOR EYESIGHT AND HEARING. THIS PUNGENT REEK SHOULD DISPERSE THEM!
SINCE WHEN DID YOU HAVE A GAS MASK?

ENOUGH TALK! SHERRY, WITH ME!

ERRM...

I THINK WE SHOULD BE SAFE HERE. SHERRY, ARE YOU OKAY?
UHH...
I'M NOT SHERRY, JAKE!
KWAME? YOU'RE DRAPED IN TOILET PAPER! WHERE ARE THE OTHERS?!

LOU--
LOUIS... STOP
FOR A WHILE...
I'M TIRED...
HUUUH...

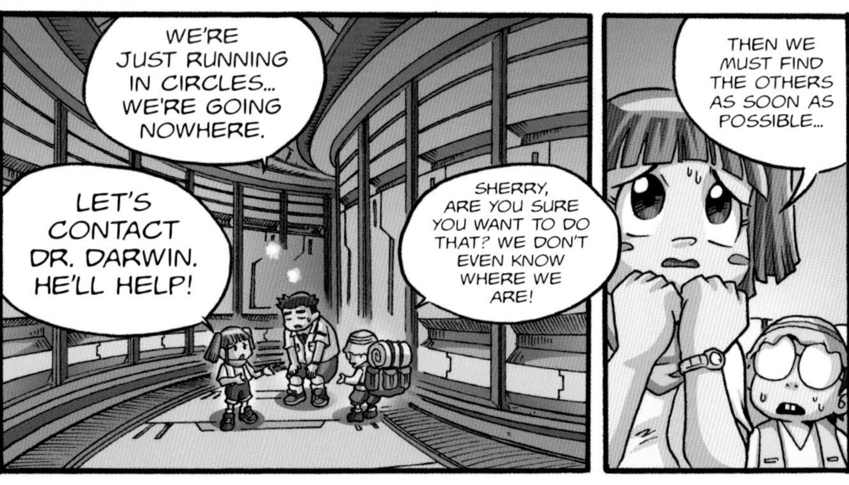

WE'RE JUST RUNNING IN CIRCLES... WE'RE GOING NOWHERE.
LET'S CONTACT DR. DARWIN. HE'LL HELP!
SHERRY, ARE YOU SURE YOU WANT TO DO THAT? WE DON'T EVEN KNOW WHERE WE ARE!
THEN WE MUST FIND THE OTHERS AS SOON AS POSSIBLE...

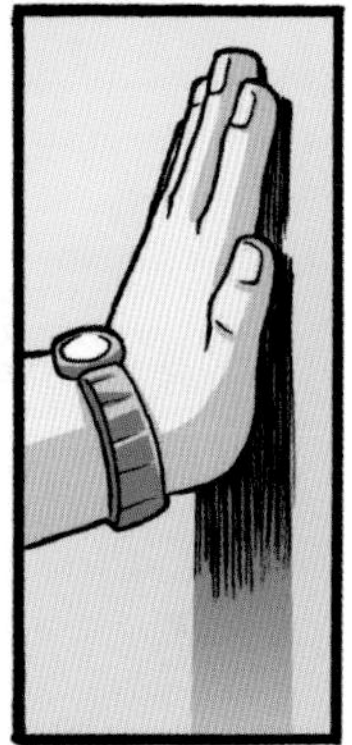

DON'T WORRY, SHERRY. I'M HERE.

I'LL GET US OUT OF THIS PLACE SAFE AND SOUND!

AN HOUR LATER...

I'm exhausted... Louis, is that the exit?
YES! YES! THERE'S LIGHT HERE. THIS MUST BE THE EXIT!

HA! HA! HA! FINALLY! WHAT TOOK YOU ALL SO LONG?!

HA! HA!
HA! HA!
HA! HA!
HA! HA!

Conservation Status

Extinct	Extinct in the Wild	Critically Endangered	Endangered	Vulnerable	Near Threatened	Least Concern
EX	EW	CR	EN	VU	NT	LC

Species: Ailuropoda melanoleuca
Length (including tail): 4 to 6 feet
Weight: 165 to 353 pounds
Diet: Bamboo
Distribution: China
Habitats: Bamboo forests

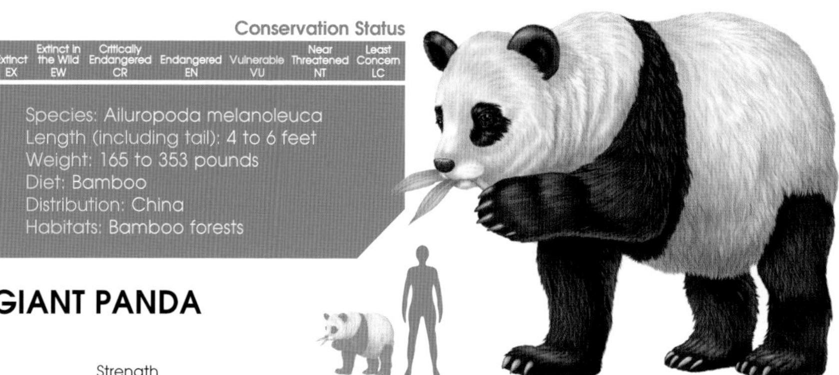

GIANT PANDA

Strength
Speed
Intelligence
Defense
Attack

Unmistakable with its black ringed eyes and black-furred legs, pandas are unlike any other bear species. Although they are carnivorous, their diet is almost 99% bamboo. Due to their low nutrient diet, pandas have to consume between 20 to 31 pounds of bamboo per day to sustain themselves and live very sedentary lives to conserve energy. Pandas have also developed a unique "thumb" on their forepaws to grip the bamboo as their powerful jaws tear off succulent shoots.

SLOTH BEAR

Conservation Status

Extinct	Extinct in the Wild	Critically Endangered	Endangered	Vulnerable	Near Threatened	Least Concern
EX	EW	CR	EN	VU	NT	LC

Species: Melursus ursinus
Length (including tail): 4.5 to 6.25 feet
Weight: 121 to 423 pounds
Diet: From fruits and honey to termites
Distribution: India, Sri Lanka, Bangladesh, Bhutan, Pakistan, and Nepal
Habitats: Lowland forests

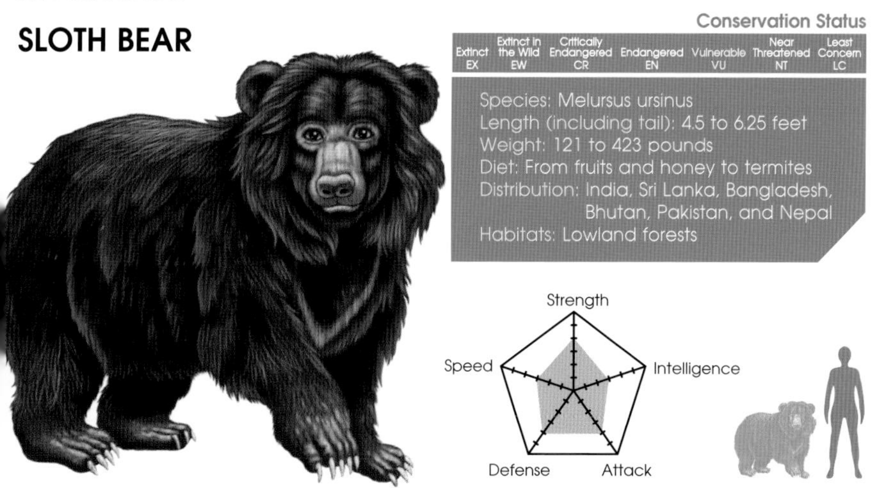

Strength
Speed
Intelligence
Defense
Attack

Found mostly across the Indian subcontinent, sloth bears are good climbers that feed mostly on termites, honey, and fruits. With powerful curved claws, they can easily break apart termite mounds to locate their favorite food. Characterized by black shaggy fur, especially around the head, mother bears often regurgitate half-digested jackfruit and honeycombs to feed their cubs. This dark yellow mass, known as "bear's bread," is considered a delicacy by some locals.

BORNEAN ORANGUTAN

Conservation Status

Extinct EX	Extinct In the Wild EW	Critically Endangered CR	Endangered EN	Vulnerable VU	Near Threatened NT	Least Concern LC

Species: Pongo pygmaeus
Length: Up to 5.75 feet
Weight: 86 to over 260 pounds
Diet: From fruit to slow lorises (rarely)
Distribution: East Malaysia and Indonesia
Habitat: Tropical and subtropical rainforest

Male Bornean orangutan

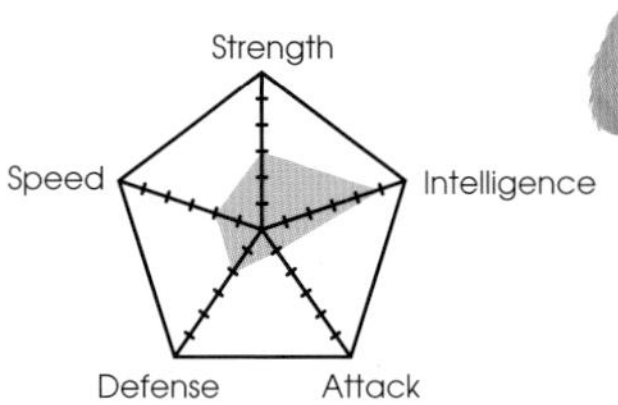

Both the Bornean and Sumatran orangutans are great apes. With genes similar to ours, they are intelligent social animals and are capable of using tools and are quite gentle-natured. Although they spend most of their time in trees, orangutans are also active on the ground because they are not considered primary prey by local carnivores.

◀ To get to the ants within, orangutar and chimpanzees will insert a stic into the nest, allowing the ants t crawl onto the stick which they w then remove and lick clean.

DID YOU KNOW?

Orangutan, which: in Malay means, "person of the forest" represents one of the recognized Malay compound nouns for animals incorporated into the English language.

CHAPTER 4
MAD DOC IN THE HOUSE

RESEARCH CENTRAL
DOCTOR, INTELLIGENCE SHOWS THAT JAKE AND THE TEAM ARE AT THE YELLOWSTONE NATIONAL PARK.

AND IMAGES TAKEN FROM OUR SATELLITE MOMENTS AGO...

...SHOW A SUSPICIOUS BUILDING IN THE PARK. IT SEEMS ALL THE SMUGGLED ANIMALS ARE IN THERE.

COULD IT BE HIM?

HELLO, KIDS, WELCOME TO MY RESEARCH LAB. ARE YOU IMPRESSED BY THE SCALE OF IT?

I THINK IT'S THIS WAY, GUYS.
HEY! ARE YOU LISTENING?

STAY WHERE YOU ARE! I'M NOT DONE WITH YOU!
WHATEVER

KILLER STARE!
What's this?
A koala bear!

WHOA... TAKE IT EASY, OKAY? MY MOM ALWAYS SAID DON'T PLAY WITH KNIVES, LET'S NOT BE HASTY, EH?

WELL, NOW THAT I HAVE YOUR ATTENTION!

OKAY! YOU WIN! SO, PUT THAT CHOPPER DOWN ALREADY, HUH?!

TAZEN?!

GUYS, LOOK! HE'S HERE!

UMM... WHAT'S SO SPECIAL ABOUT THE TWO ORANGUTANS?

?
?
YOU MUST BE SEEING THINGS!
ARE YOU BLIND?

SO... YOU GUYS KNOW THAT LITTLE WILD KID WHO CAN COMMUNICATE WITH ANIMALS?
HMM... I THINK I RECOGNIZE OUR CAPTOR!

JUST WHO IS THIS NUT?
NOW I RECALL!

WORLD GEOGRAPHIC
ISSUE 03
WILDLIFE DIGEST
YOU'RE **DOCTOR CHARLES!** THE AWARD-WINNING ZOOLOGIST RENOWNED FOR CONSERVATION WORK AROUND THE WORLD!
BUT YOU MYSTERIOUSLY WENT MISSING A WHILE BACK. WHAT HAPPENED?

AND WHY ARE YOU DOING THE THINGS WHICH YOU FOUGHT SO HARD AGAINST?

CLAP
CLAP
WELL DONE. WELL DONE. YOU KNOW YOUR STUFF, SQUIRT!

ALL MY LIFE, I'VE WITNESSED THE TERRIBLE THINGS THAT PEOPLE DO TO ANIMALS AROUND THE WORLD!
WHAT HAVE ANIMALS DONE TO US? WE DESTROY THEIR HABITATS. WE KILL THEM FOR OUR OWN PLEASURE. WITHOUT REMORSE! WITHOUT A SHRED OF CONSCIENCE!

THESE ANIMALS DON'T STAND A CHANCE AGAINST US...

WELL, IT'S TIME FOR PAYBACK!

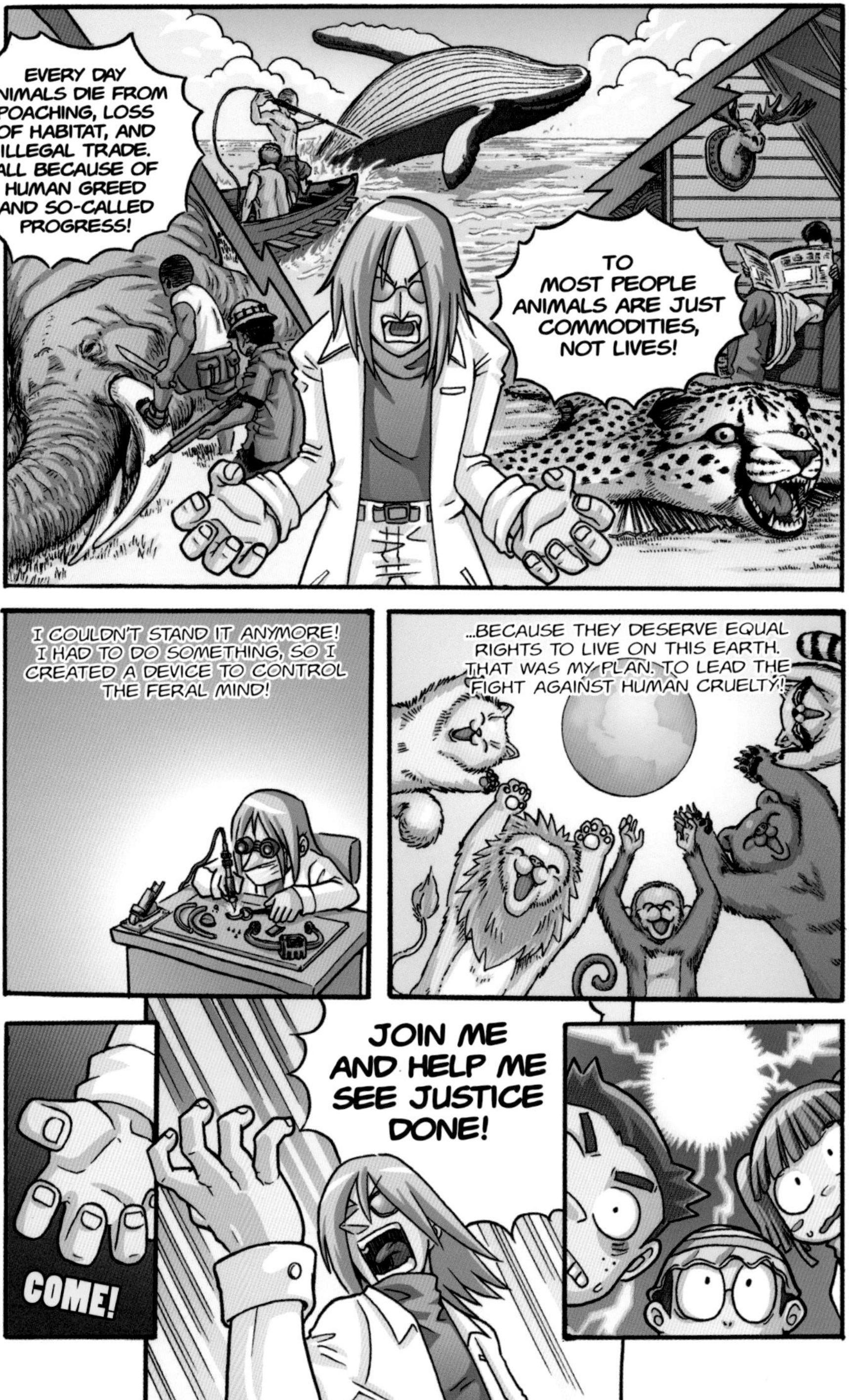

EVERY DAY ANIMALS DIE FROM POACHING, LOSS OF HABITAT, AND ILLEGAL TRADE. ALL BECAUSE OF HUMAN GREED AND SO-CALLED PROGRESS!

TO MOST PEOPLE ANIMALS ARE JUST COMMODITIES, NOT LIVES!

I COULDN'T STAND IT ANYMORE! I HAD TO DO SOMETHING, SO I CREATED A DEVICE TO CONTROL THE FERAL MIND!

...BECAUSE THEY DESERVE EQUAL RIGHTS TO LIVE ON THIS EARTH. THAT WAS MY PLAN. TO LEAD THE FIGHT AGAINST HUMAN CRUELTY!

COME!
JOIN ME AND HELP ME SEE JUSTICE DONE!

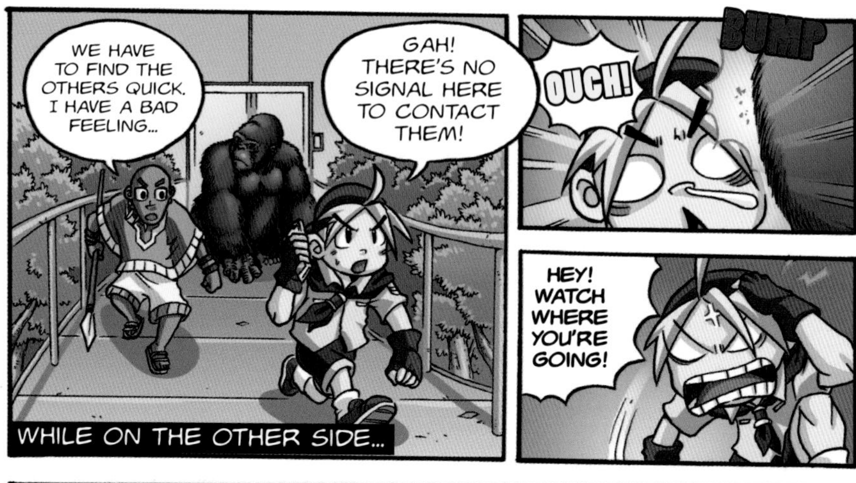
WE HAVE TO FIND THE OTHERS QUICK. I HAVE A BAD FEELING...
GAH! THERE'S NO SIGNAL HERE TO CONTACT THEM!
WHILE ON THE OTHER SIDE...
BUMP
OUCH!
HEY! WATCH WHERE YOU'RE GOING!

ACK! BEAR!
ACK! HUMAN!

HUH? IT WAS MORE SCARED THAN I WAS!

WHAT'S WRONG WITH IT?
JAKE! HOLD ON!

HEY! WHERE ARE YOU GOING, HUH?

WHY ARE YOU SO SCARED? C'MON, SHOW ME SOME SPUNK!

CAN'T "BEAR" TO FACE A KID LIKE ME, HUH?

THESE BEARS LOOK WEAK AND SICKLY...

IF I HAD TO GUESS...

THESE MUST BE ASIAN BLACK BEARS CAPTURED FOR THEIR BILE.
THE WOUNDS ON THEIR ABDOMENS AND DULL EYES ARE THE TELL-TALE SIGNS.

TO EXTRACT THE BILE, A METAL TUBE IS INSERTED INTO THE GALLBLADDER OF A BEAR CONFINED IN A VERY SMALL CAGE. THIS EXTREMELY PAINFUL PROCESS OFTEN CREATES INFECTIOUS WOUNDS WHICH CAUSE DISEASES. WHICH LOWER THEIR LIFE EXPECTANCY TO AROUND A THIRD OF WILD BLACK BEARS.

BUT WHY WOULD ANYONE WANT THEIR BILE?

"BLACK BEAR BILE IS BELIEVED TO HAVE HEALING PROPERTIES. BUT RESEARCH HAS SHOWN IT CAN BE SUBSTITUTED WITH HERBS OF SIMILAR MEDICINAL VALUE."

I DIDN'T EXPECT YOU TO KNOW THIS MUCH, JAKE. YOU KNOW YOUR STUFF!

GOTCHA! I WAS ACTUALLY READING FROM THE ANALYZER!

DON'T WORRY, MY FRIENDS!

I PROMISE YOU THAT I WILL...
...SEE TO IT THAT THEY PAY!

?
?
?
?

SO, ARE YOU WITH ME... OR AGAINST ME?

LOUIS, DON'T TELL ME YOU AGREE WITH WHAT HE JUST SAID!

I THINK HE'S RIGHT. MOST PEOPLE ARE ACTUALLY HARMING ANIMALS INSTEAD OF PROTECTING THEM.

LOUIS! HAVE YOU FORGOTTEN WHAT DR. DARWIN TAUGHT US?

...

AH, I SEE. YOU'RE STUDENTS OF THE GREAT DARWIN. I USED TO RESPECT HIM BUT HE HAS GONE SOFT!

MAYBE DR. DARWIN IS NOT WHAT HE USED TO BE... BUT YOU'RE NOT HALF THE MAN HE IS!
!

WHY DON'T YOU JOIN US TO CREATE A BETTER WORLD FOR BOTH HUMANS AND ANIMALS!

HA! HA! HA! AM I BEING TOLD WHAT TO DO BY A BUNCH OF KIDS? HOW AMUSING!

SINCE WE CANNOT REACH AN AGREEMENT...

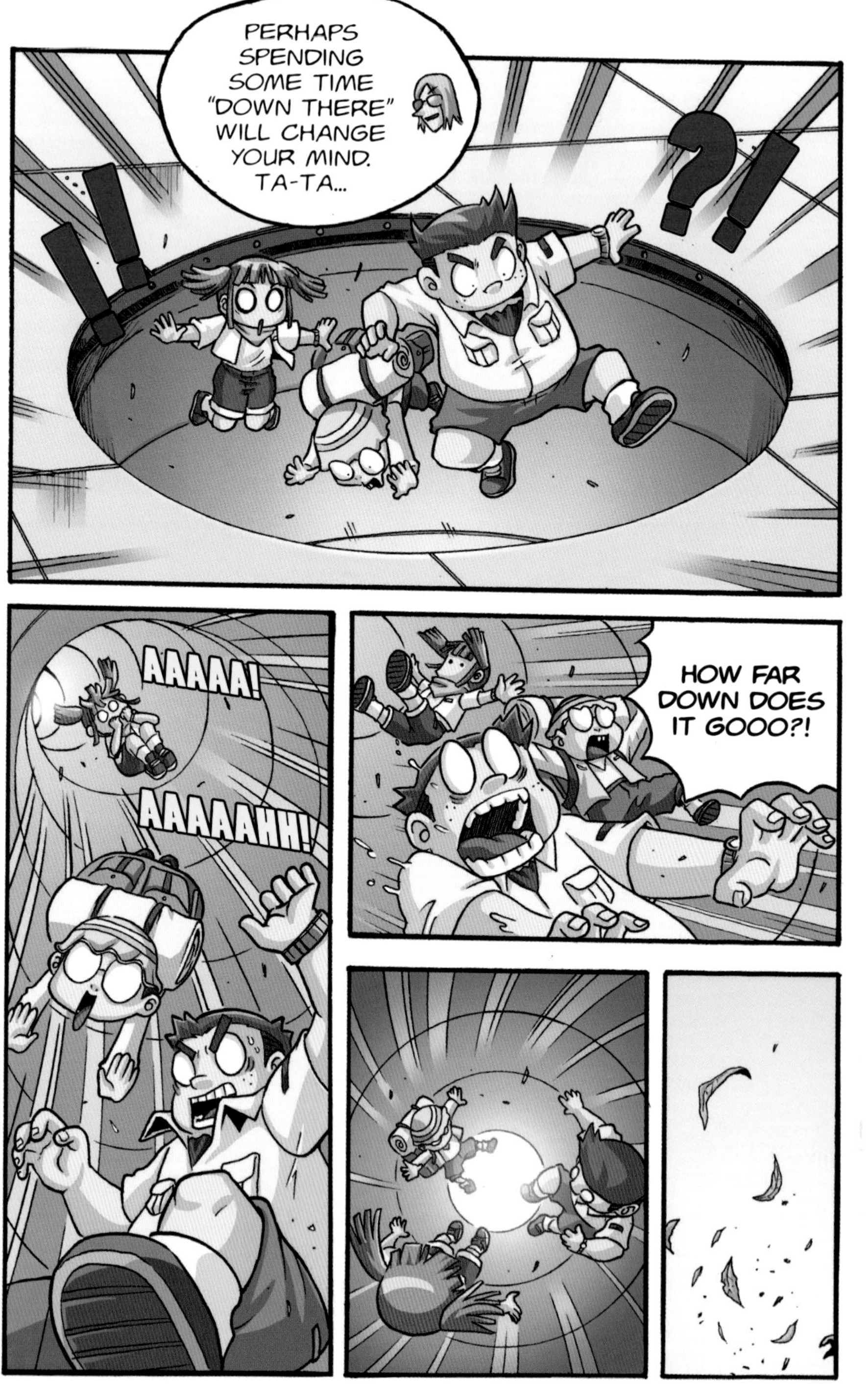

PERHAPS SPENDING SOME TIME "DOWN THERE" WILL CHANGE YOUR MIND. TA-TA...

?!

!!

PHEW... WHERE ARE WE?

WAAAIT! WHERE'S BEAN?!

HEY! HOW DID YOU END UP THERE?
MMF! G-GET... O-OFF ME YOU... HIPPO!

DOHK

WHAT IS THIS THING?

BWEK
AWW, SO CUTE! A COMMON SQUIRREL MONKEY! I CAN'T BELIEVE IT'S REALLY THIS SMALL!

Gross! Yuck!

UH-OH! WHITE-HEADED CAPUCHINS! THEY DON'T SEEM TO BE VERY HAPPY...

LET'S GET A MOVE ON BEFORE THE MONKEY BUSINESS STARTS!
RUUUUN!
EEEK!
POK
PAAP
AAA!
OWW!

CLEVER BULLIES! HITTING US FROM UP IN THEIR TREES!
GAH, THOSE HAIRY LITTLE MONSTERS! OWW!

CAN YOU CONTACT JAKE AND KWAME?
NO, THERE'S NO SIGNAL HERE!
HUH?!
EXACTLY! I HAVE INSTALLED SIGNAL JAMMERS IN THIS BUILDING. NO ONE CAN CONTACT THE OUTSIDE WORLD... EXCEPT ME!

HA HA HA! HOW DO YOU LIKE MY MONKEY PUZZLE?

ARE YOU ALL ENTERTAINED BY MY FURRY FRIENDS?

THIS GUY IS REALLY TWISTED!

Conservation Status

Extinct EX	Extinct in the Wild EW	Critically Endangered CR	Endangered EN	Vulnerable VU	Near Threatened NT	Least Concern LC

Species: Saimiri sciureus
Length (including tail): 2 to 2.5 feet
Weight: 1 to 2.4 pounds
Diet: From fruits to small vertebrates
Distribution: Central & South America
Habitats: Tropical rainforests

COMMON SQUIRREL MONKEY

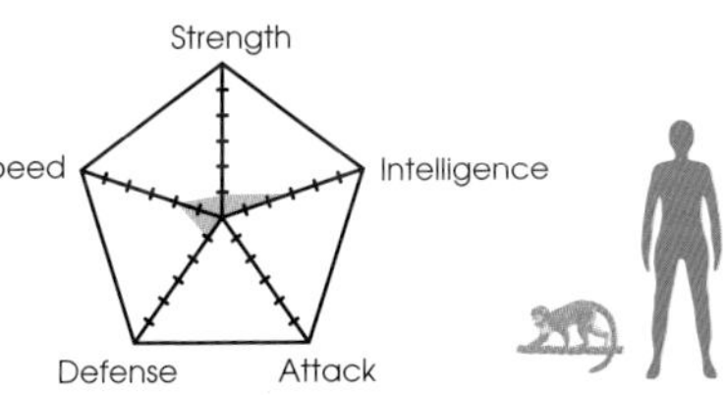

Common squirrel monkeys are diurnal (active in daylight) and arboreal (tree-dwellers). Most are of least concern in terms of conservation except for the Central American and Black squirrel species. Often kept as pets or for research; they usually live in large groups of up to 500 individuals. Hunted by falcons, snakes, and jaguars, they have to move rapidly with their long tails acting as "balancing poles."

Conservation Status

Extinct EX	Extinct in the Wild EW	Critically Endangered CR	Endangered EN	Vulnerable VU	Near Threatened NT	Least Concern LC

Species: Cebus capucinus
Length (including tail): 1.8 to 3.3 feet
Weight: Up to 9 pounds
Diet: From fruits to small vertebrates
Distribution: Central America & Northwestern South America
Habitats: Tropical forests

WHITE-FACED CAPUCHIN

A highly intelligent monkey, the capuchin is known to utilize tools as weapons or to get food and will rub plants on its body to deter parasites and insects. They are sometimes trained to perform tricks and assist people who are severely disabled. As social creatures in the wild, they live in groups of about 20 males and females and display various ways of communicating from loud calls, facial expressions to scent marking by rubbing urine on their feet.

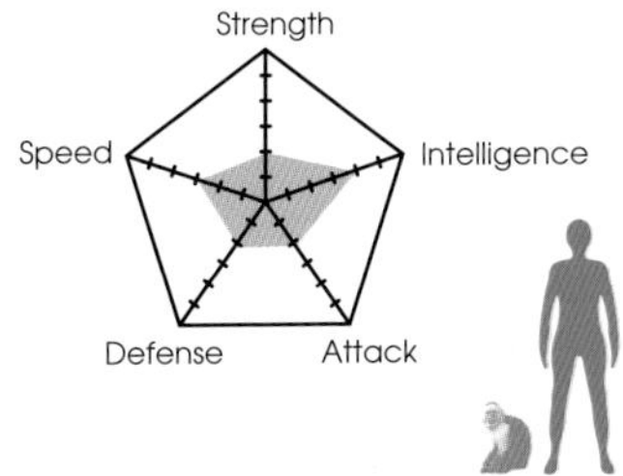

Conservation Status

Extinct EX	Extinct in the Wild EW	Critically Endangered CR	Endangered EN	Vulnerable VU	Near Threatened NT	Least Concern LC

Species: Lemur catta
Length (including tail): 3.1 to 3.6 feet
Weight: Average 5 pounds
Diet: From fruits to small vertebrae.
Distribution: Southern Madagascar
Habitat: From scrubland to mountainous forests.

RING-TAILED LEMUR

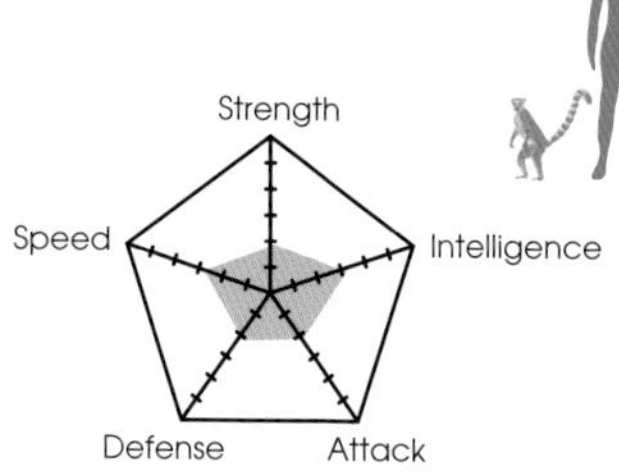

Distinguished by its long bushy black-and-white ringed tail, the lemur can only be found in Madagascar. Highly sociable, they live in groups of up to 30 which are female-dominated. As part of their social-bonding ritual, lemurs huddle together or sunbathe by sitting upright facing the sun and employ a range of vocalizations to communicate.

Conservation Status

Extinct EX	Extinct in the Wild EW	Critically Endangered CR	Endangered EN	Vulnerable VU	Near Threatened NT	Least Concern LC

Species: Nycticebus coucang
Length (including tail): 1 to 1.25 feet
Weight: 1.3 to 1.5 pounds
Diet: From tree sap to insects
Distribution: Southeast Asia
Habitat: Tropical rainforests

SUNDA SLOW LORIS

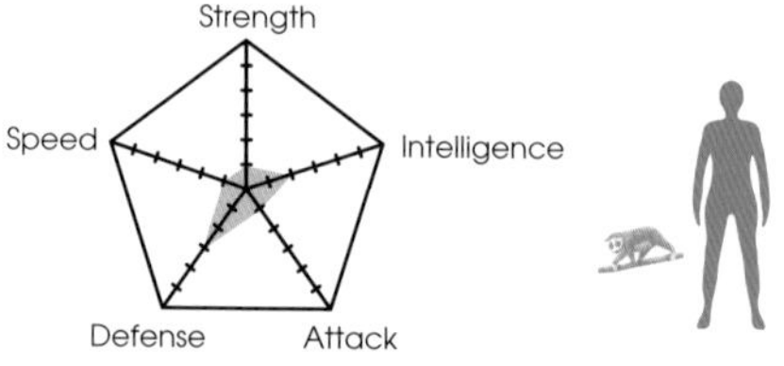

The slow loris is a nocturnal primate that possesses large reflective eyes for better night vision. Unlike most primates that live in groups, this one is usually solitary. Due to its slow movement, one way to protect itself from threats is by covering its fur with toxins secreted from glands found on the insides of its elbows. In the wild, the slow loris is seen as non-aggressive, and may exhibit a monogamous (single partner) social behavior.

CHAPTER 5

MONKEY MAYHEM!

WUU UUH UUH
URRRCH... SO NOISY!
WUU OOH OOH
WUU WUU WUU
AAH AAH

ENOOOUGH! WE KNOW WE'RE TRESPASSING. NO NEED TO KICK UP SUCH A FUSS! MY EARS!

WUU CHII
WUU CHII

CHII CHII CHII

JAKE?!

CEASE YOUR CATERWAULING!
KO

WOW! SHERRY'S GOT SOME MOJO. SHE KAYOED IT WITH ONE PUNCH!
BIG MISTAKE...

NOW ITS FRIENDS ARE COMING AFTER US! WE BETTER GET OUT OF HERE.
SORRY... I THOUGHT IT WAS JAKE. SOUNDED LIKE HIM TOO...

HUH? IT'S STARTING TO RAIN!

NO, IT'S NOT! THEY'RE PEEING ON US! EEEEEW... GROSS!

WUUU!
WUU
AAAAH!

OH, NO--?!
Not me again?!

SHERRY, DON'T WORRY. I'LL PROTECT YOU!
LOUIS!
MANTLED HOWLERS WILL ATTACK WITH THEIR URINE AND FECES WHEN PROVOKED.
PEE AND POO?!

SHERRY, ARE YOU OKAY?
I'M... FINE, BUT WHAT ABOUT BEAN?

GET AWAY, POO-BOY!

Hey! Wait for me!
DON'T COME TOO CLOSE! YOU NEED A SHOWER, BEAN, SERIOUSLY!

WHOA...

A WHITE-FACED SAKI FAMILY...

WOW! WHAT A BEAUTIFUL BLACK-AND-WHITE COLOBUS!

.AND THE
HILIPPINE
TARSIER!
...WHICH LOOKS LIKE ME... HA HA!

THIS ONE IS A POTTO. IT HAS A DISTINCT ODOR THAT SMELLS LIKE CURRY!

THE AYE-AYE HAS LONG, THIN FINGERS.

YIPES! I'M LOST. I WONDER WHERE THE DETOUR HAS BROUGHT ME...

SNIFF... THAT'S SULPHUR. WHERE'S IT COM--

-IIIING!
SPLASH

A HOT SPRING INSIDE A RESEARCH LAB?!

OH! A JAPANESE MACAQUE!

WOW! I'VE NEVER SEEN A MACAQUE THAT BIG BEFORE!

HI, BEAN! THERE YOU ARE!

THE HOT SPRING SMOOTHES MY SKIN. AHH, BLISS...
C'MON, BEAN, GET IN!

OOOO... THIS IS HEAVENLY...
Aaaahh...

HEY! THIS IS NOT THE TIME TO RELAX! TAZEN NEEDS OUR HELP!

WUU AAH
WUU AAH

THERE'S A COMMOTION OVER THERE. COULD BE THE OTHERS...
WUU AAH
WUU AAH

HEEK!
WHOOP!

WHOA! MONKEY CIVIL WAR! INCREDIBLE!
WAARK!
NRUH!

THE OLIVE BABOON PLATOON ON THE LEFT!
AND THE MANDRILL HORDE ON THE RIGHT!

GWAK! SHEEK!

EEEEEEK!
WOOK!

BWEEEEK!
WARK!

KILLER BITE!

NYARK!
NYARK!
THE RED BUM MONKEY WON! WOOHOOO!
?
?
SSSHH!
WE SHOULD BE SAFE IN THERE, SO WE CAN PLAN OUR NEXT MOVE!
STOP! DON'T GO IN THERE!
THERE'S NOTHING IN THERE... IT'S WHERE I KEEP MY JUNK, THAT'S ALL!
OOOOH... JUNK, EH?
I FORBID YOU!

SORRY, DOC, TOO LATE. YOU'VE PIQUED OUR CURIOSITY!
VOOOSH

KIDS NOWADAYS NEVER LISTEN TO ADULTS ANYMORE, SIGH!

HUH?!
Haa!

GUYS... YOU FOUND ME! THANK YOU! BUT... BRING FOOD? I'M STARVING!

JEEEZ, TAZEN, EVEN IN THIS SITUATION, ALL YOU THINK ABOUT IS FOOD...

GLAD YOU'RE FINE, TAZEN. BUT HOW ARE WE GOING TO RELEASE YOU WITHOUT JAKE?

ACK, THIS CRIMINAL SKILLS THING IS NOT COOL!
GUESS IT'S UP TO ME NOW!

BEHIND YOU!

SHERRY, LOOK OUT!

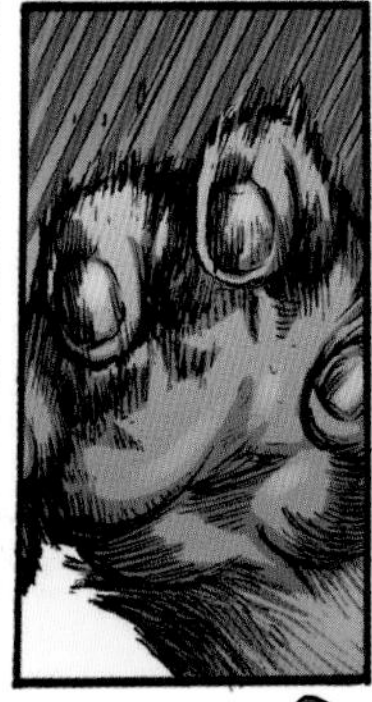

WOOOK!

WUAK! GARK! BWA HUGAAH!
WUUH! WUUH!
<THEY'RE MY FRIENDS, DON'T HURT THEM!>
IT ISN'T LISTENING TO TAZEN! ITS THAT HOKEY HEADGEAR!
GET BEHIND ME I'LL DEAL WITH IT!
BRING IT ON, HAIRBALL!
WHOOOOK!
NOOO! PLEASE... NO... PIPE!

HEE
YAH!

SHIEEEEK!

DON'T...
MY
DAAAAD!

WHA--?
YOUR
DAD?!

LOUIS,
WATCH
OUT!

KA-TANG

CRASH
BOOM
BANG

GUYS... DAD... STOP FIGHTING... STOP!

SMACK
PAAP

SO! YOU WANNA PLAY ROUGH?

THIS IS HOW YOU DO IT!

THE LOUIS HOOK PUNCH!

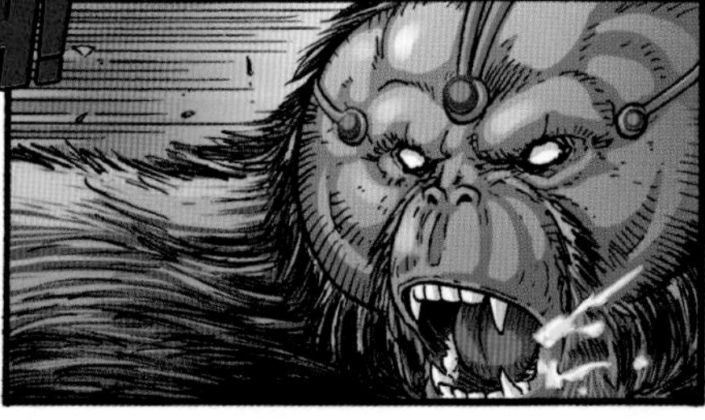

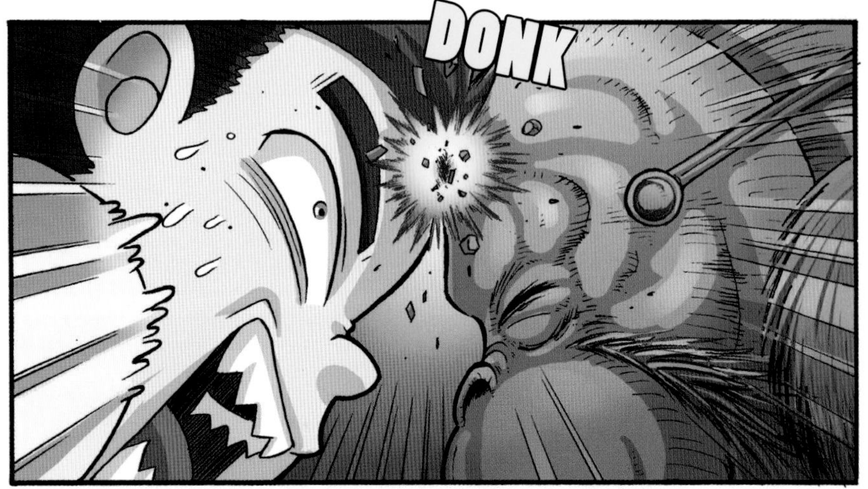
DONK

HEAD HOODOO... GONE! DAD... OKAY!

EXIT
LET'S GO, GUYS.
LET'S FIND JAKE AND KWAME!

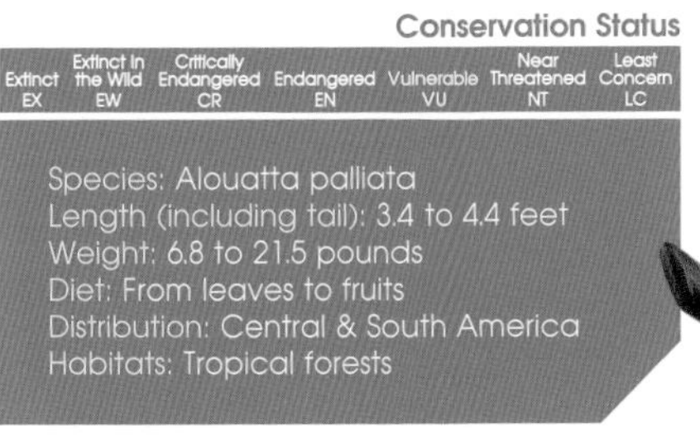

Conservation Status

Extinct	Extinct in the Wild	Critically Endangered	Endangered	Vulnerable	Near Threatened	Least Concern
EX	EW	CR	EN	VU	NT	LC

Species: Alouatta palliata
Length (including tail): 3.4 to 4.4 feet
Weight: 6.8 to 21.5 pounds
Diet: From leaves to fruits
Distribution: Central & South America
Habitats: Tropical forests

MANTLED HOWLER

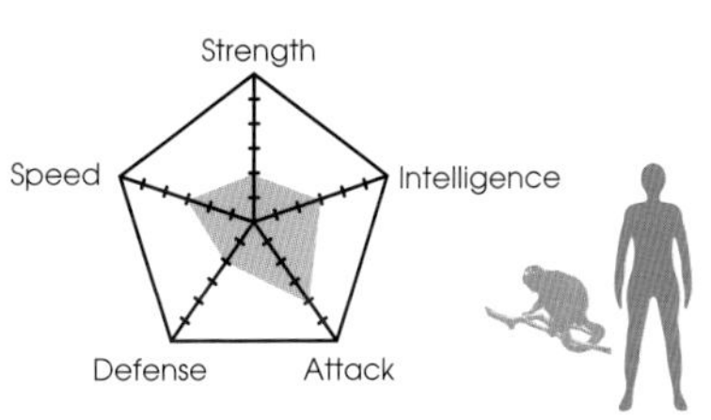

This New World monkey is one of the most common and largest primates in Central America, and gets its name from its loud "howling" calls that can be heard miles away. Its movement is aided by a long prehensile tail that can grab onto branches. They spend most of their time sleeping/resting despite being diurnal. A group (or troop) is dominated by an alpha-male which sometimes kills the offspring of other males to ensure its own young remain with the group.

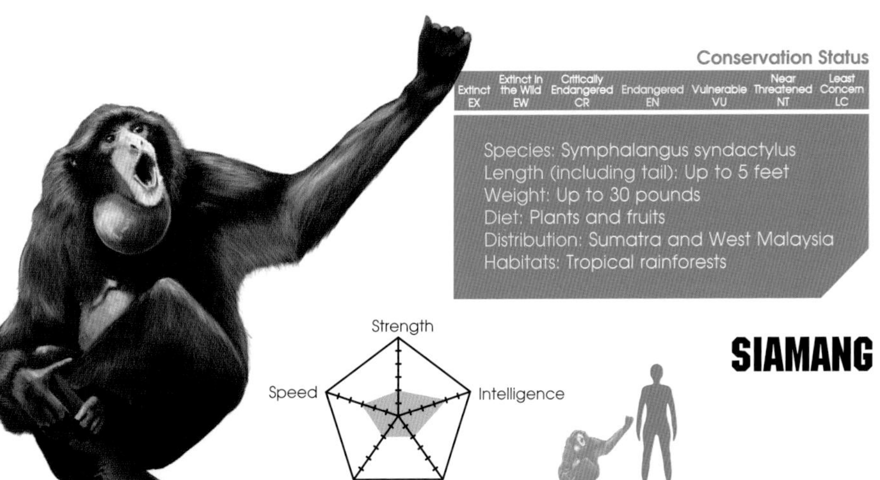

Conservation Status

Extinct	Extinct in the Wild	Critically Endangered	Endangered	Vulnerable	Near Threatened	Least Concern
EX	EW	CR	EN	VU	NT	LC

Species: Symphalangus syndactylus
Length (including tail): Up to 5 feet
Weight: Up to 30 pounds
Diet: Plants and fruits
Distribution: Sumatra and West Malaysia
Habitats: Tropical rainforests

SIAMANG

The siamang's most distinctive feature is its gular sac — a throat pouch that can be inflated to the size of its own head — allowing it to make loud, resonating calls. The largest of the lesser apes, this tailless primate is generally known to be monogamous (having one partner) and has been observed grooming its mate extensively. Although it is arboreal, it sometimes walks on all fours upon the forest floor.

TARSIER

Conservation Status

Extinct EX	Extinct in the Wild EW	Critically Endangered CR	Endangered EN	Vulnerable VU	Near Threatened NT	Least Concern LC

Species: Tarsiidae
Length (including tail): 3.5 to 6.3 inches
Weight: 2.8 to 5.8 ounces
Diet: Insects
Distribution: Borneo, Sulawesi, Sumatra, and the Philippines
Habitat: From scrubland to rainforests

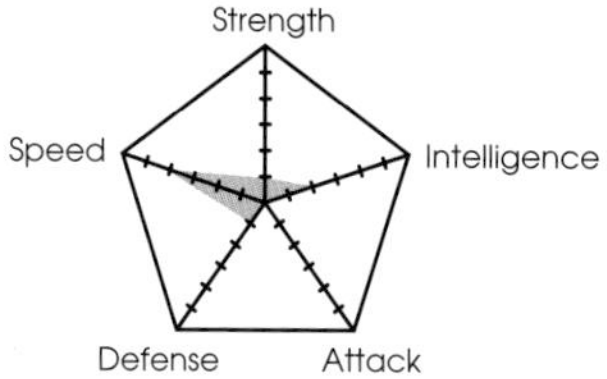

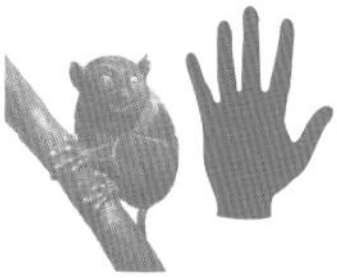

Strength
Speed
Intelligence
Defense
Attack

Tarsiers are one of the smallest primates in the world, characterized by their huge bulging eyes and unusually long ankle bones. Because the eyes are fixed to their sockets, they must turn their entire head (up to 180°) to look around. Tarsiers are nocturnal predators that hunt mostly insects, notably grasshoppers and crickets, which they locate using their acute sense of sight and hearing. Tarsiers are shy solitary creatures that do not live well in captivity with their average lifespan possibly reduced by half if removed from the wild.

POTTO

Conservation Status

Extinct EX	Extinct in the Wild EW	Critically Endangered CR	Endangered EN	Vulnerable VU	Near Threatened NT	Least Concern LC

Species: Perodicticus potto
Length (including tail): 1 to 1.6 feet
Weight: Up to 3.3 pounds
Diet: From tree sap to insects
Distribution: Central and Western Africa
Habitat: Tropical rainforests

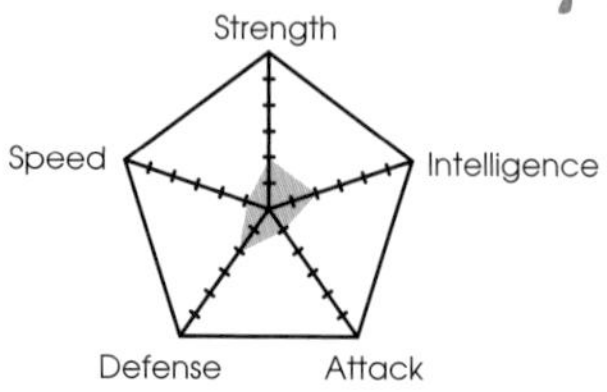

Strength
Speed
Intelligence
Defense
Attack

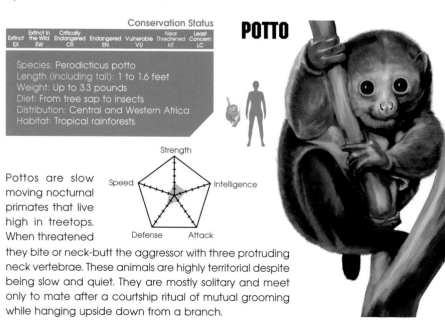

Pottos are slow moving nocturnal primates that live high in treetops. When threatened they bite or neck-butt the aggressor with three protruding neck vertebrae. These animals are highly territorial despite being slow and quiet. They are mostly solitary and meet only to mate after a courtship ritual of mutual grooming while hanging upside down from a branch.

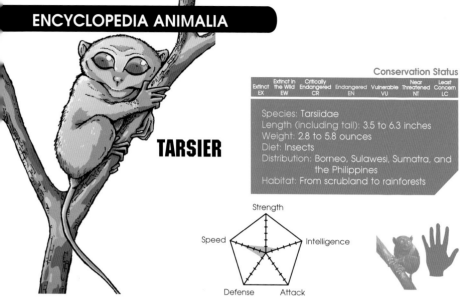

CHAPTER 6

ICE TO MEET YOU

FOG DESCENDS ON THE JUNGLE

CHEW
CHEW
CHEW

HEY, BIG FELLA. STOP EATING, WILL YA?

ARE YOU THINKING WHAT I'M THINKING?
I THINK IT WANTS US TO EAT THE LEAVES.
TH-THANKS... BUT WE'RE NOT HUNGRY. YOU CAN HAVE IT.
OKAY... WE'LL EAT!

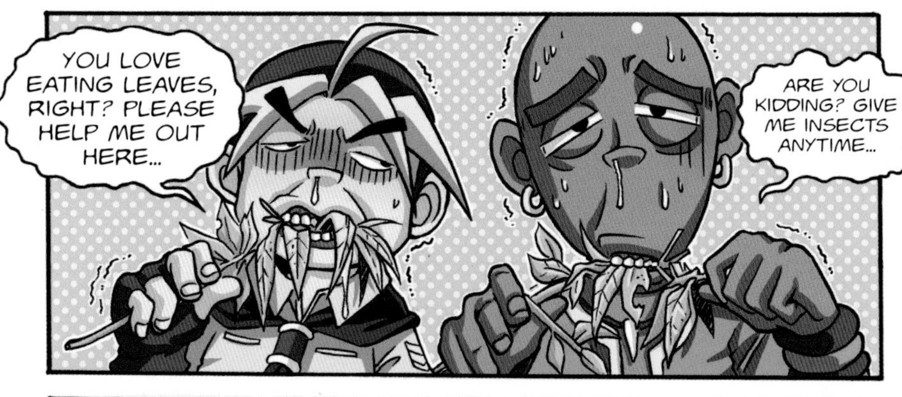
YOU LOVE EATING LEAVES, RIGHT? PLEASE HELP ME OUT HERE...
ARE YOU KIDDING? GIVE ME INSECTS ANYTIME...

BARF
BLURF

AAAAH... ACAI BERRIES! THOSE ARE DELICIOUS!

THAT'S A NICE-LOOKING BEAR! LOOKS LIKE THE START OF A BEAUTIFUL FRIENDSHIP BETWEEN THEM.
Clak
REALLY....?

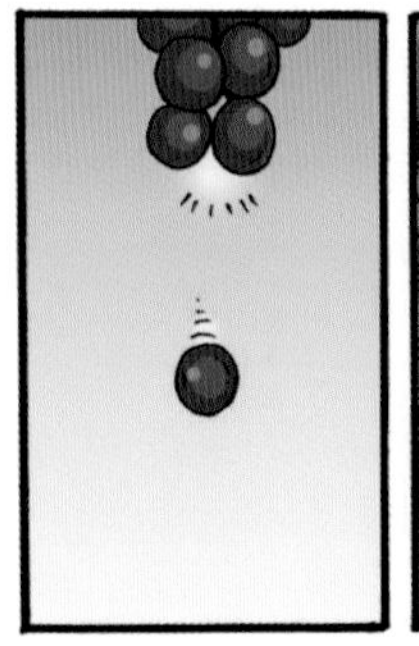

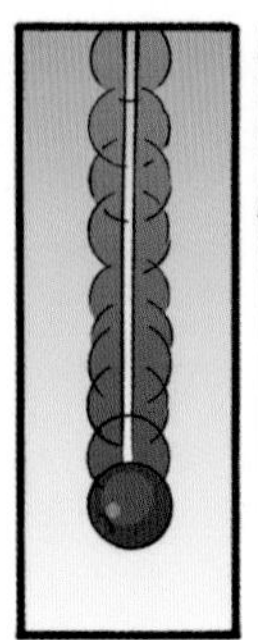

YEAH! AND ALL IT TOOK WAS ONE BERRY O END THE RIENDSHIP!

POK
KTSH

HA!
HA!
OMM!
NOM!
NOM!

Uuuh! That was good!

LOOK! A DOOR, IT MIGHT BE THE EXIT!
FOOOSH

WOWOWEE! IT'S A WINTER WONDERLAND!

BRRRR... OKAY... MY BAD. IT'S F-FREEZING...

SNIFF
Let's get outta here, now!
SNIFF
SNIFF

IT'S BEEN A WHILE SINCE I SKATED. LET ME SHOW YOU GUYS MY NIFTY MOVES!
WHA...

JAKE, I THINK WE MAY BE IN DANGER...

GRRRROWR
GRRRRR!
POL... POLAR BEEEAR! HEEEELP!

WOOOH!
AAAAH---
AAAAH---
WEEEE...
TWO-FOOTED KICK!

OH, NO! THERE GOES THE DOOR!
GROWR!
C'MON, KONG! FLOAT LIKE A BUTTERFLY! STING LIKE A BEE!
NO PROBLEM!

HEAD SLAM!

KONG IS DOWN!

POLAR BEARS ARE FEROCIOUS CARNIVORES KNOWN TO ATTACK HUMANS. DESPITE ITS HUGE SIZE, IT MOVES FAST AND TAKES DOWN PREY USING POWERFUL FRONT PAWS WHILE ITS BITE FORCE CAN REACH 1323 POUNDS PER SQUARE INCH!

NOW'S NOT THE TIME!

GROWL!

JAKE, I CAN'T SKATE. SAVE YOURSELF!

JAKE, FASTER! FASTER! IT'S GETTING CLOSER!
THUM
KRRRRRAK
CRAAK
CRAK
CRAK

SAY YOUR PRAYEEERS!
KRAKOOM
IT FELL THROUGH THE ICE!
IT DROWNED! SAYONARA, POLAR BEAR!
ALL CLEAR, HERE WE GO-- OOF!
LOOK! ANOTHER DOOR! LET'S GET OUTTA THIS FROZEN WASTE!

IT'S TOO COLD... THE LOCK IS FROZEN SOLID...
KRAK
KRAK
JAKE, DID YOU HEAR THAT? I THINK IT'S...
?
...IT'S NOTHING. IT'S ALL IN YOUR MIND!
DON'T BREATHE DOWN MY NECK, WILLYA? GIMME SOME ROOM.
KRRAAAK

GARRGH!

IT DIDN'T DROWN! THIS IS IT. WE'RE DOOMED!
JAKE, THE LOCK... THE LOCK!

DROP

HELP ME FIND THE PIN!

KA-DUP
KA-DUP

RAAH!
COME ON, PIN, WHERE ARE YOU?!

GROWL!

KONG MANAGED TO OPEN THE DOOR AND I COULDN'T! THIS IS EMBARRASSING!
NOW'S NOT THE TIME, JAKE! RUN!

DOOR
CLOSING!

KA-THUNG

ARRH!

That was
too close...

Conservation Status

Extinct EX	Extinct in the Wild EW	Critically Endangered CR	Endangered EN	Vulnerable VU	Near Threatened NT	Least Concern LC

Species: Papio anubis
Length (including tail): 2.9 to 5.6 feet
Weight: 22 to 81.5 pounds
Diet: From plants to small primates
Distribution: Central Africa
Habitats: From grasslands to desert areas and rainforests.

OLIVE BABOON

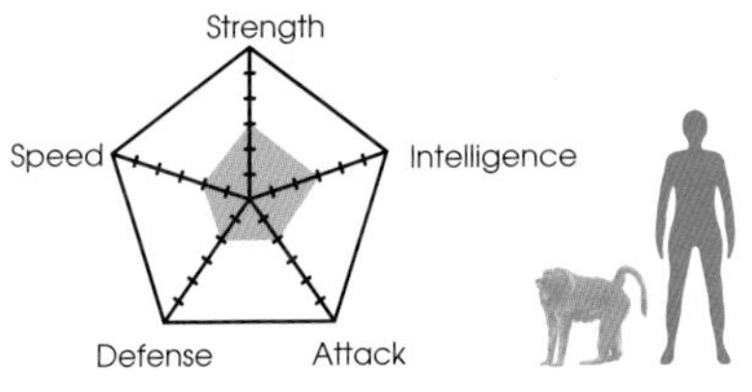

These baboons can be found in 25 equatorial African countries. Active during the day, they forage in groups of between 15 and 150 individuals, with more females than males. Males gain dominance through fighting while female ranking is hereditary. When groups become too large, they will break up to ensure less competition for limited resources. Baboons do not require much conservation attention because they are highly adaptable and eat almost anything they can find.

MANDRILL

Conservation Status

Extinct EX	Extinct in the Wild EW	Critically Endangered CR	Endangered EN	Vulnerable VU	Near Threatened NT	Least Concern LC

Species: Mandrillus sphinx
Length (including tail): 2 to 3.5 feet
Weight: 22 to 81.5 pounds
Diet: Fruits, plants, and insects
Distribution: Western Africa (Cameroon, Gabon, Guinea, and Congo)
Habitats: Tropical rainforests

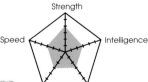

Strength
Speed
Intelligence
Defense
Attack

Closely related to baboons, mandrills are the largest species of monkey, displaying a strikingly colored snout and rear; the former striped blue, the latter a rosy scarlet. They are often found in sprawling groups, or hordes, as large as over 800, mostly foraging by day and sleeping in trees by night. Adult males usually stand their ground when threatened and bear their sharp canine teeth which can measure 2.5 inches length.

JAPANESE MACAQUE

Conservation Status

Extinct EX	Extinct in the Wild EW	Critically Endangered CR	Endangered EN	Vulnerable VU	Near Threatened NT	Least Concern LC

Species: Macaca fuscata
Length (including tail): 2 to 2.2 feet
Weight: 18.5 to 25 pounds
Diet: From roots to fish
Distribution: Japan
Habitat: Deciduous, broadleaf, and evergreen forests

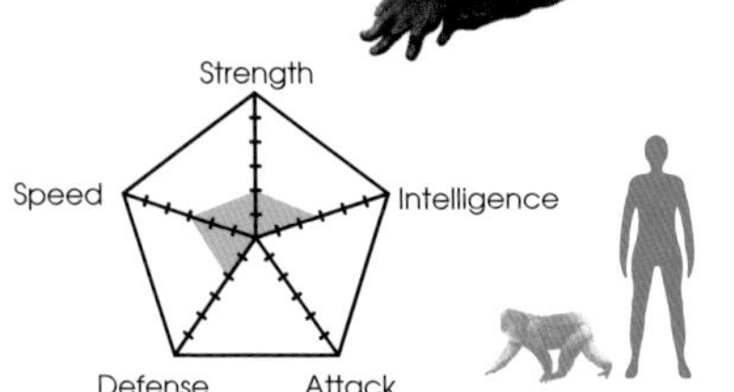

Strength
Speed
Intelligence
Defense
Attack

The snow monkey is the most northern-living primate in the world and can cope with temperatures as low as -4 °F. These Old World monkeys spend considerable time soaking in hot springs and grooming each other to strengthen bonds. Troops are female-dominant and can contain several generations of related females while males move out to form their own troops when they reach maturity.

Conservation Status

Extinct EX	Extinct in the Wild EW	Critically Endangered CR	Endangered EN	Vulnerable VU	Near Threatened NT	Least Concern LC

Species: Rhinopithecus roxellana
Length (including tail): 3.1 to 4.5 feet
Weight: 25.5 to 40 pounds
Diet: From leaves to fruits
Distribution: Central & southwest China
Habitat: Highland/coniferous forests (1 to 2 miles above sea level)

Strength
Speed
Intelligence
Defense
Attack

GOLDEN SNUB-NOSED MONKEY

Being hunted for their beautiful golden fur and body parts for Chinese medicinal use, plus habitat loss have contributed to this Old World monkey's decline. These diurnal primates are able to withstand severe cold weather and form small mixed-gender groups. When threatened, they band together to form a larger troop to repel their enemies.

CHAPTER 7

SCRATCH YOU LATER!

DOC, YOU AIN'T LETTIN' 'EM GET AWAY, EH?

"BEAR" WITH ME, THEY WON'T GET FAR!

GRAAAR!

I THINK THIS STAIRWAY WILL LEAD US TO THE EXIT!
AAUUH!

WHA--?!

FROM MY YEARS OF EXPERIENCE, WE CAN SAVE TIME AND ENERGY BY TAKING THE ELEVATOR!
...

DON'T BE SO LAZY, LOUIS. YOU PROBABLY NEED THE EXERCISE!
YEAH, YEAH, SHUDDUP, FRODO!
...

THAT'S... THE BEAR... THAT ATTACKED US!
A BROWN BEAR, STANDING ON ITS HIND LEGS CAN REACH OVER 9 FEET TALL...
WAAA... BEARS ARE NOT SUPPOSED TO BE IN ELEVATORS!
STOP TAKING PHOTOS, BEAN! I NEED HELP HERE!
...IT CAN ALSO SUSTAIN SPEEDS OF 35 MPH FOR MORE THAN 10 MINUTES!

LOUIS, DON'T WORRY! CALM DOWN. JUST PLAY DEAD!
REALLY?

A LITTLE BIT OF KETCHUP SHOULD DO IT!
PLOP

WAIT A MINUTE!

GET UP! GET UP! DON'T PLAY DEAD! IT'S TOO LATE NOW!

!!

YOU MORON! IF I GET EATEN, I'LL KILL YOU!

HOW TO DIFFERENTIATE BETWEEN BROWN BEARS AND AMERICAN BLACK BEARS

- BROWN BEARS ARE BIGGER.
- BROWN BEARS HAVE HUMPED BACKS.
- THE BROWN BEAR HAS A ROUNDER, SHORTER HEAD.

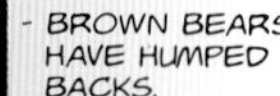

GRRR
JUMMM
NEVER MIND THAT, BEAN! JUST TELL ME WHAT TO DO!

RUUUUN! AVOID ITS PAWS! THEY WILL BE THE END OF YOU!

NOOOO... I'M TOO YOUNG TO DIIIIIE!

ZING

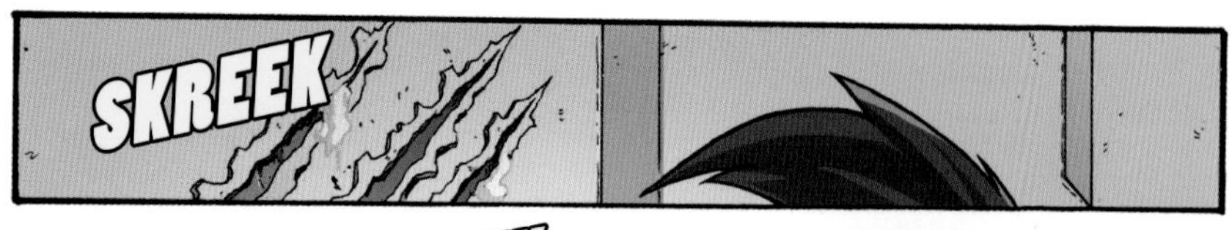
SKREEK

CHEIK

AAAAHH...

LOUIS... YOU SAVED DAD... NOW MY TURN!

BEEP
BEEP
BEEP

FINALLY, WE HAVE A SIGNAL!

LET'S CLIMB TO THE ROOFTOP! THE SIGNAL SHOULD BE STRONGER UP THERE.

WE'LL CALL THE DOC AND TELL LOUIS AND THE REST TO MEET US UP THERE.

HUK

WHOA...

I'LL NEVER TAKE HEIGHTS FOR GRANTED AGAIN! THE VIEW FROM HERE IS AMAZING!
Contact the Doctor now!

HELLO, DOC. WE'RE AT YELLOWSTONE NATIONAL PARK LOOKING FOR TAZEN, BUT WE'RE IN TROUBLE RIGHT NOW...

...WE NEED YOUR HELP ASAP!

I INSTRUCTED YOU ALL TO COME BACK, BUT YOU IGNORED MY ORDERS.
?!

TAKE THIS AS A LESSON TO NEVER REPEAT THE SAME MISTAKE AGAIN.

BEEP--

OKAY, ALRIGHT, DOC! IF YOU'RE NOT GONNA HELP. I'LL BRING THE TEAM BACK MYSELF!
THONG
YES! THAT'S THE WAY, JAKE!
WHAT HAPPENED TO ALL THAT BRAVADO?
...

MOOOVE! THE BROWN BEAR IS RIGHT BEHIND ME!

LOUIS, SHERRY, BEAN! AND TAZEN!

YEAAAA! WE'RE BACK TOGETHER AGAIN!

GGRRRR

GRRUH!
HUUMPF...

TOO LATE! IT'S HERE!
GRRROWL!
WHAT DID YOU GUYS DO TO ANGER IT?!

RAAH
THUD

GREAT TO SEE YOU AGAIN, TAZEN, WE WERE ALL WORRIED ABOUT YOU!
ERRMM... THANK YOU...

WELL. THE BROWN BEAR IS RENOWNED FOR ITS STRENGTH, IT CANNOT BE EASILY DEFEATED!

LET THE SHOW BEGIN!

IT'S A PITY FOR YOUR GORILLA THOUGH! ALL IT TAKES IS ONE DIRECT HIT FROM A PAW... OR ONE VICE-LIKE BITE, AND IT'S ALL OVER!
UHH! DON'T COUNT YOUR CHICKENS YET! KONG IS NO PUSHOVER!
...
MAD SCIENTIST HAIR, WHAT A CLICHÉ!
!!
GROAR!

GRAA!
WHMP

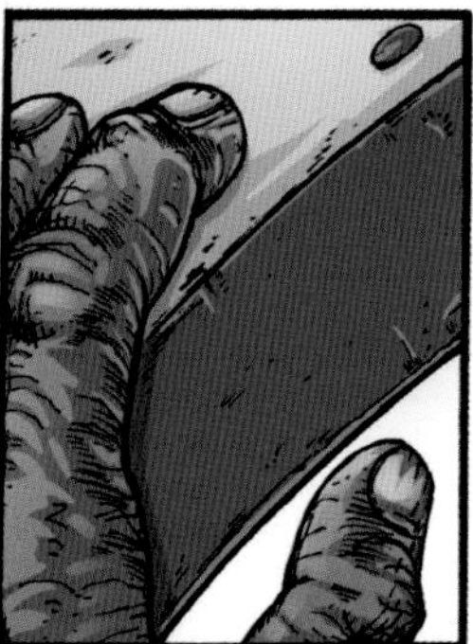

BAAAM

WAY TO GO, KONG! TEACH THAT BEAR A LESSON!

SMART! IT'S USING THE STEEL DOOR AS A SHIELD!
THRAM

THANG

THONG

HE'S DEFENSELESS NOW!

NGUM
PERHAPS I UNDER-ESTIMATED THE BEAR'S FEROCITY!
DANG! THAT IS ONE BLOODY FIGHT!
STOP!
OVER HERE, YOGI! HAVE SOME ACAI BERRIES!
GRRR...
?

LUCKILY YOU HAVE SOME. BROWN BEARS ARE OMNIVOROUS AND THEY LOVE TO EAT FRUITS AND BERRIES, BESIDES FISH AND MEAT.

NOM!
NOM!

HEY! ATTACK NOT SNACK!

GRUH!

GGRRRR!
AAAAAAH!
Jake!

Conservation Status

Extinct EX	Extinct in the Wild EW	Critically Endangered CR	Endangered EN	Vulnerable VU	Near Threatened NT	Least Concern LC

Species: Ursus maritimus
Length (including tail): 6 to 9.8 feet (up to 10.8 feet tall standing)
Weight: 330 to 1543 pounds. (Reaching 1764 pounds during winter)
Diet: Seal, fish, carrion
Distribution: The Arctic Circle
Habitats: Polar wastes, tundra

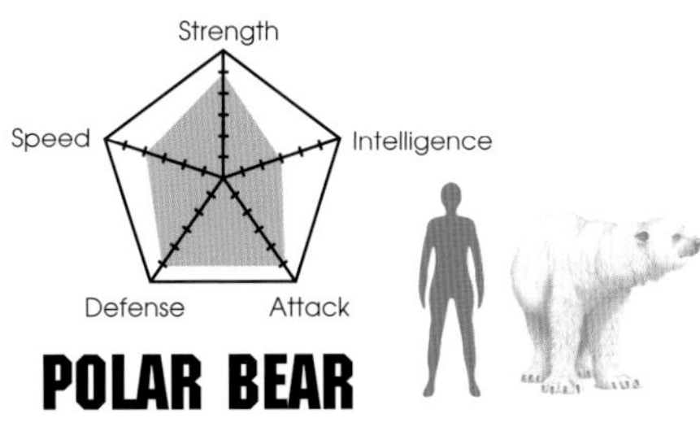

POLAR BEAR

Found only in the frigid North Polar region, polar bears are the largest land carnivores in the world. They have large paws (up to 1 foot wide) ideal for walking on ice and a thick white coat with a layer of blubber (up to 4 inches) for insulation against sub-zero temperatures. They feed mostly on seals, which they usually catch by waiting at sea ice openings where seals surface to breathe. Polar bears are excellent swimmers, and can be spotted swimming as far as 220 miles from land. They do not hibernate and can fast for up to 8 months by using stored fat as energy. They rarely attack humans unless severely provoked or hungry and unlike brown bears, are not territorial.

Aggression

Fights among polar bears usually occur during mating season in April or May. They tend to be intense and often cause severe injuries. At other times, Polar bears appear to shy away from conflict.

When threatened, it rears upright on its hind legs, snarling to intimidate antagonists, in the hopes of averting conflict.

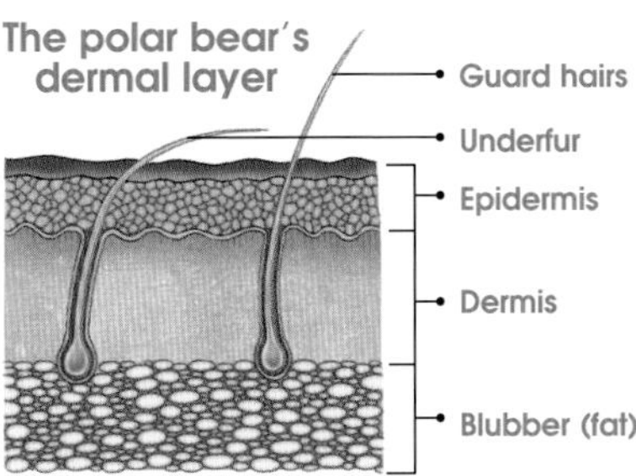

Fat - A 4 inch blanket.

Epidermis - Darker in color to absorb more heat.

Underfur - Prevents heat from escaping.

Guard hairs - Long, transparent, oily and hollow, they are waterproof and look white in sunlight. They also help in maintaining buoyancy.

DID YOU KNOW?

The polar bear's liver is poisonous to eat due to excessive amounts of vitamin A from consuming seals, their main source of food.

Conservation Status

Extinct	Extinct in the Wild	Critically Endangered	Endangered	Vulnerable	Near Threatened	Least Concern
EX	EW	CR	EN	VU	NT	LC

Species: Tremarctos ornatus
Length (including tail): 4.25 to 7 feet
Weight: 77 to 440 pounds
Diet: Fruits, cactus, crops such as sugarcane and corn
Distribution: Northwestern South America
Habitat: Mountainous areas, scrub deserts, and cloud forests

SPECTACLED BEAR

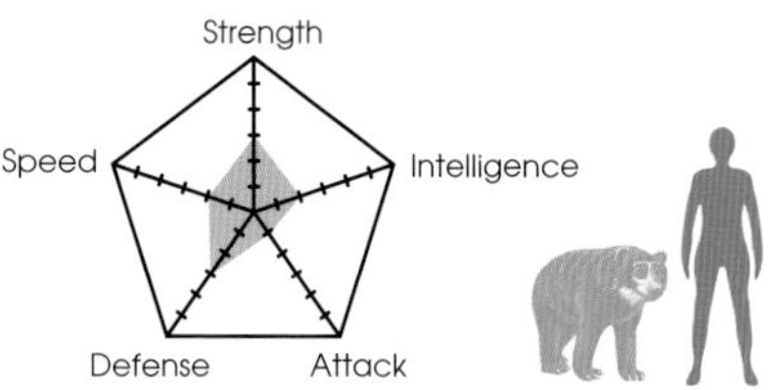

The only native South American bear, it is distinguished by beige-colored "spectacle" markings. Being solitary, it often climbs trees to avoid humans and other bears, to rest, and to also store food. This mid-sized bear is more herbivorous compared to other bears (except the panda) with meat comprising only around 7% of its diet. It is also non-territorial and relatively docile in nature.

Conservation Status

Extinct	Extinct in the Wild	Critically Endangered	Endangered	Vulnerable	Near Threatened	Least Concern
EX	EW	CR	EN	VU	NT	LC

Species: Ursus thibetanus
Length (including tail): 4.3 to 6.76 feet
Weight: 143 to 441 pounds
Diet: From grasses to medium-sized mammals.
Distribution: Southwest to Southeast Asia
Habitat: Mountains to sea level mixed forests, desert

ASIAN BLACK BEAR

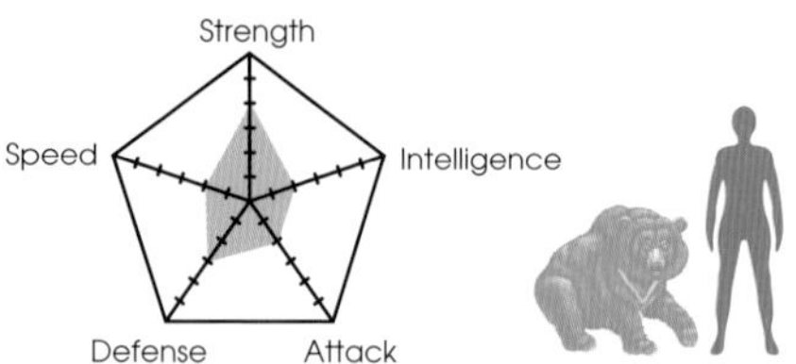

Also known as the moon or white-chested bear due to its distinctive whitish half-moon chest markings. Largely herbivorous and arboreal, it is a prolific forager, eating almost anything it can find from insects to domestic livestock. It is also the most bipedal of all bears, and can walk upright for nearly one-third of a mile. Usually shy and cautious, they can nevertheless be very aggressive towards humans.

CHAPTER 8
THE ULTIMATE SACRIFICE

GRRRR!

TAZEN'S DAD!
HMMMMPH!
KONG!
GRRAAH!

GUH!
BAAR!
THAT WAS TOO CLOSE FOR COMFORT!

GGRRRRR!

ROAR!

SNORE
HUH? IT GOT KNOCKED OUT. HOW?
?

A TRANQUILIZER DART!

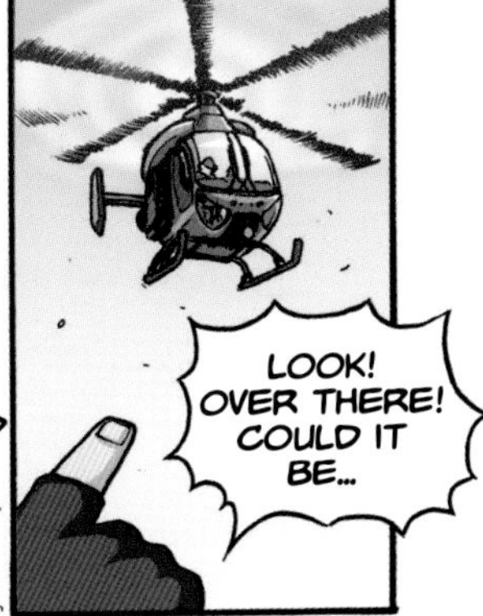
LOOK! OVER THERE! COULD IT BE...

HELLO, KIDS! I HOPE YOU'VE LEARNED YOUR LESSON. ALWAYS STICK TO THE PLAN!

DR. DARWIN! **MR. SMITH!** YOU CAME JUST IN TIME! YIPEEE!

IT'S BEEN A LONG TIME, CHARLES, DID YOU REALLY THINK YOUR CRAZY PLAN WOULD WORK?
THE TWO GUYS WITH HIM ARE THE POACHERS WHO ESCAPED FROM SIBERIA!

WHY DO YOU OPPOSE ME, PROFESSOR?!
ANSWER ME!

PROFESSOR?! WAS HE THE DOC'S STUDENT?!

TAKA TAKA TAKA TAKA
I WILL NEVER AGREE WITH YOUR VIEWS BECAUSE THEY'RE AGAINST THE LAWS OF NATURE.
IT'S UNCONSCIONABLE TO USE TECHNOLOGY TO CONTROL THESE CREATURES!
ANIMALS MUST BE PROTECTED, NOT CONTROLLED!

LOOK AT THESE KIDS, THEIR UNDERSTANDING OF ANIMALS IS MUCH DEEPER THAN YOURS. SINCERITY MATTERS, DR. CHARLES.
You'll be alright.
You da man!

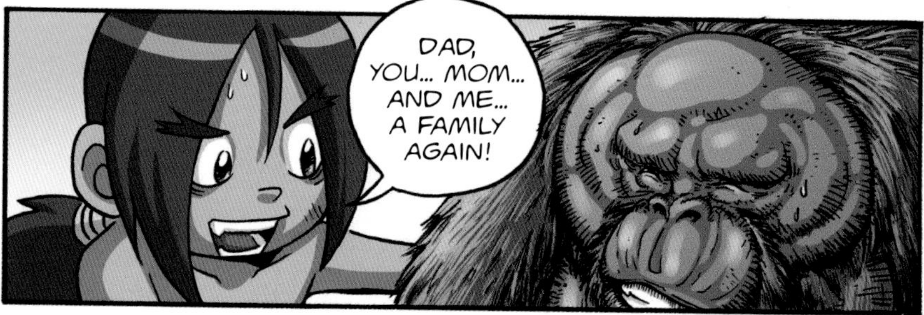
DAD, YOU... MOM... AND ME... A FAMILY AGAIN!

GIVE IT UP, CHARLES!
IT'S NOT TOO LATE TO MAKE THINGS RIGHT AGAIN. WE CAN FIND BETTER WAYS TO HELP THE ANIMALS. YOU AND ME!

TAKA
TAKA
TAKA
TAKA
SORRY, PROF, THE SOUND OF YOUR CHEST FLEXING DEAFENED ME!
YOU PUNK!

HA HA HA...

GGRRRR!

WATCH OUT! IT'S THE BEAAAAR!

WE TOTALLY FORGOT! IT'S GONE BERSERK!

DAD... DAAAAD!
NRUH MAH
<MY SON...>
GWAK BUH!
<...LIVE LIFE TO THE FULLEST!>
WAH!

SEE WHAT YOU'VE DONE? YOU'VE CREATED MONSTERS OUT OF THESE ANIMALS! STOP IT NOW BEFORE YOU MAKE THINGS WORSE!
ERRR... I...
NO! EVEN IF THE BROWN BEAR WAS SACRIFICED TO MAKE MY PLAN A SUCCESS, IT DIED FOR A GREATER CAUSE!
COLLATERAL DAMAGE IS AN INEVITABLE CONSEQUENCE.

RRUMMBLE
THE WHOLE BUILDING IS SHAKING... WE GOTTA GO!
TAZEN, WE CAN'T STAY HERE ANY LONGER, LET'S GO!
WARNING! WARNING!
LIFT OFF IN T MINUS ONE MINUTE! LIFT OFF...
RUMBLE RUMBLE
QUICK! EVERYONE GET IN!
KONG IS TOO BIG! HE WON'T FIT!
BOOOM

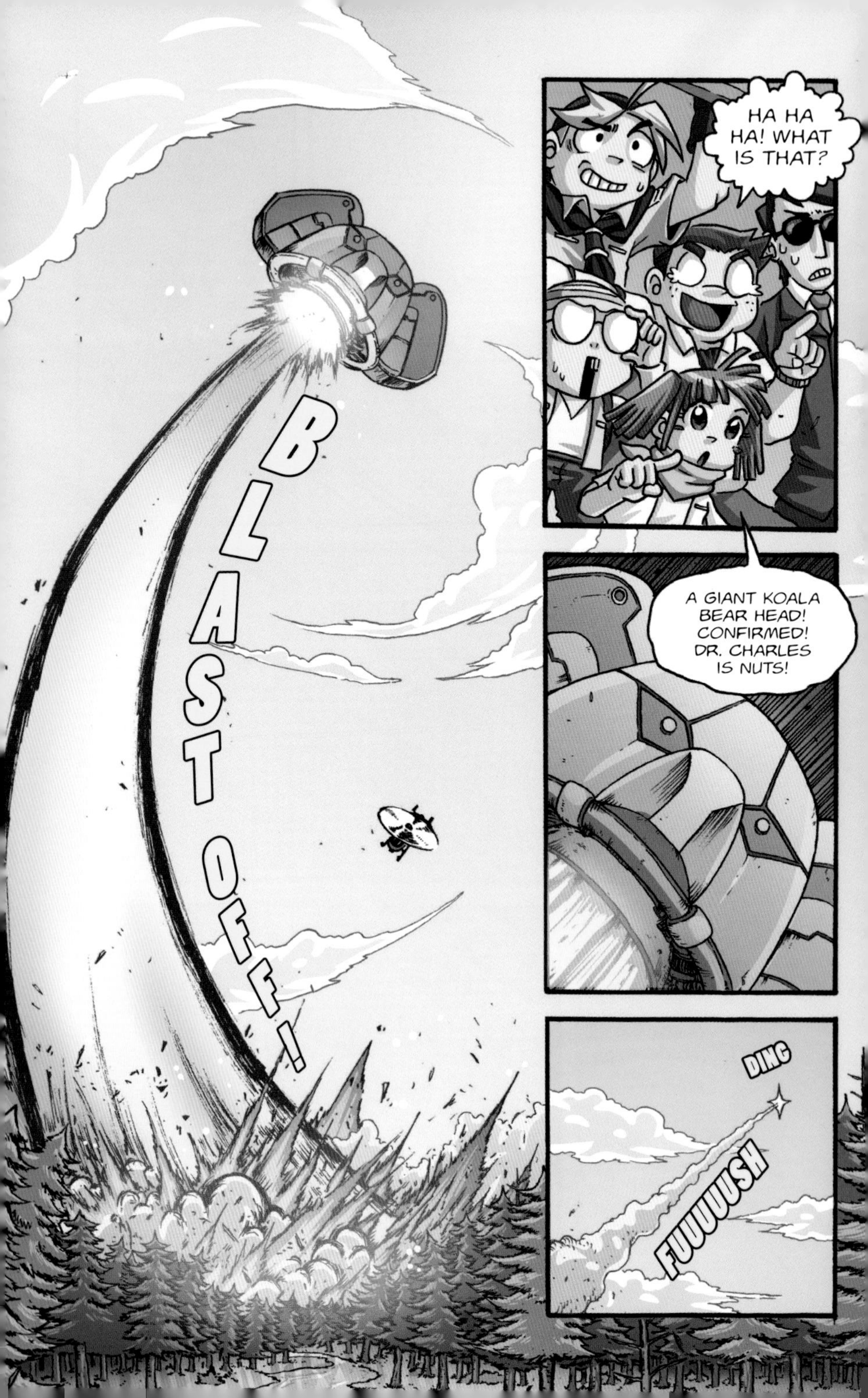
BLAST OFF!
HA HA HA! WHAT IS THAT?
A GIANT KOALA BEAR HEAD! CONFIRMED! DR. CHARLES IS NUTS!
DING
FUUUUSH

UHM...

OH, UH, DOC. WHERE'S KONG?

UNDER THE HELICOPTER, WHERE ELSE?
WHAT?! THAT'S CRUELTY TO ANIMALS!

THANK YOU FOR SAVING TAZEN. I HAVE PREPARED A FEAST FOR ALL OF YOU AS A TOKEN OF APPRECIATION!

YEAH... I'M STARVING!

COME, SIT DOWN AND EAT! DON'T BE SHY!

TAZEN...?

GUYS! TAZEN IS STILL MOURNING. SHOW A LITTLE RESPECT!

TAZEN, I KNOW THAT YOU'RE UPSET RIGHT NOW.

BUT YOU SHOULD EAT SOMETHING.

I'M SURE YOUR DAD IS PROUD OF YOU AND HIS SPIRIT LIVES ON IN YOU...

IT'S YOUR DUTY NOW. TAKE GOOD CARE OF YOUR MOM.

Eh!
Ha ha
OMM NOM

MORE! PLEASE!

VIRUNGA NATIONAL PARK, CONGO
MOUNTAIN GORILLAS ARE LED BY AN ALPHA MALE KNOWN AS A SILVERBACK DUE TO A PATCH OF SILVER HAIR ON ITS LOWER BACK. BEING THE DOMINANT MALE, THE SILVERBACK PROVIDES PROTECTION FOR THE GROUP THAT AVERAGES 10 INDIVIDUALS, AND SETTLES DISPUTES BETWEEN ITS MEMBERS.

THERE ARE NOW AROUND 880 MOUNTAIN GORILLAS LEFT IN THE WILD, MAKING THEM ONE OF THE WORLD'S MOST CRITICALLY ENDANGERED ANIMALS.

CRASH OF THE TITANS - THE END

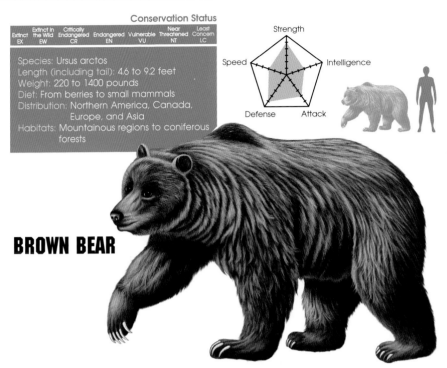

Conservation Status

Extinct EX	Extinct in the Wild EW	Critically Endangered CR	Endangered EN	Vulnerable VU	Near Threatened NT	Least Concern LC

Species: Ursus arctos
Length (including tail): 4.6 to 9.2 feet
Weight: 220 to 1400 pounds
Diet: From berries to small mammals
Distribution: Northern America, Canada, Europe, and Asia
Habitats: Mountainous regions to coniferous forests

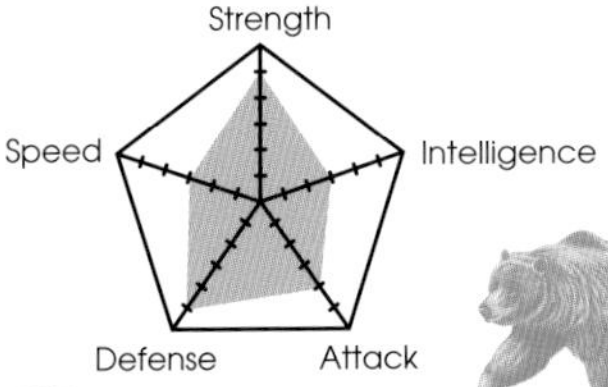

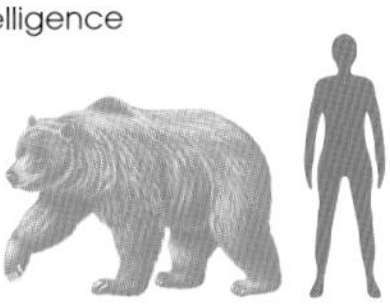

Strength
Speed
Intelligence
Defense
Attack

BROWN BEAR

Also known as the Grizzly bear in North America, it has a humped knot of muscle on its back that gives it added strength for digging. Despite its huge size, brown bears are able to run at over 31 miles per hour for more than ten minutes. Due to habitat loss and human encroachment, encounters between bears and humans are becoming increasingly common.

◀ Brown bears love salmon. When they spawn in the autumn, the bears will gather upriver to snare leaping salmon as they struggle upriver to their spawning grounds.

DID YOU KNOW?

The Alaskan brown bear or Kodiak bear is the largest brown bear species and rivals the polar bear for the title of largest terrestrial carnivore.

GORILLA

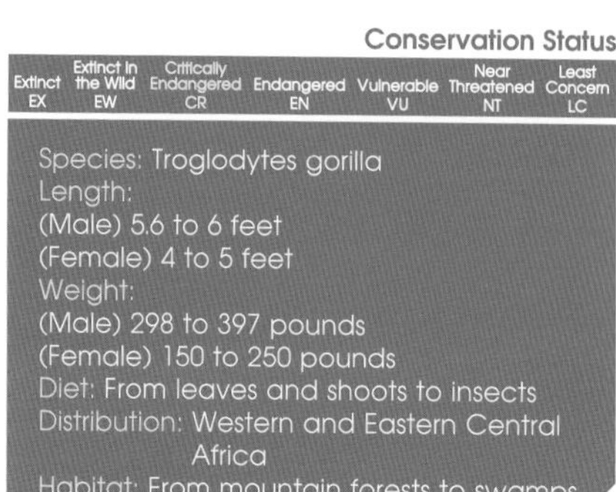

Species: Troglodytes gorilla
Length:
(Male) 5.6 to 6 feet
(Female) 4 to 5 feet
Weight:
(Male) 298 to 397 pounds
(Female) 150 to 250 pounds
Diet: From leaves and shoots to insects
Distribution: Western and Eastern Central Africa
Habitat: From mountain forests to swamps

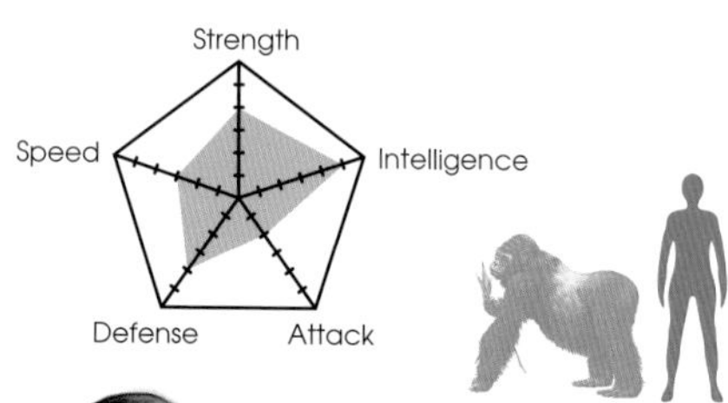

Male gorilla

The Gorilla is the largest living primate and comprises of two species, each with two subspecies – the mountain and lowland gorillas. The lead male is also known as a silverback due to the distinctive silvery hair around the small of its back that develops upon maturity. Although gorillas look menacing, they are reclusive creatures that live in small troops and forage for vegetation during the day.

A gorilla troop typically includes a silverback, several mature females, and their offspring. As the leader, the silverback is responsible for protecting its members; leading them in search of food and mediating conflicts between members. Gorillas are highly intelligent and exhibit some human traits such as the capacity to laugh, grieve, develop friendships, use tools, and exhibit a preference for colors.

◀ When two silverbacks meet, they will intimidate each other by beating their chests, thumping the ground, and baring their sharp canine teeth. Fighting is avoided if possible.

◀ Gorillas have a unique way of getting around called knuckle-walking – where they fold their palms in and use their knuckles for support when moving forward.

EXERCISE

01 **Which of the following animals is not a bear?**

A. Giant panda **B.** Koala **C.** Polar bear

02 **Bears rely on ______ to search for food.**

A. Eyesight **B.** Hearing **C.** Smell

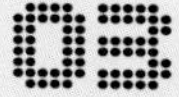

Giant pandas are carnivorous but they do not consume much meat. Why?

A. Their teeth are not sharp

B. They are not able to prey on other animals

C. They no longer enjoy the taste of meat due to the loss of certain genes

What is the function of a siamang's large gular sac?

A. To make loud and resonating sounds

B. To threaten enemies

C. To attract the opposite sex

05 **Why do brown bears gather upstream in autumn?**

A. To feast on salmon that spawn during that season

B. They need to bathe to prepare for winter

C. Water is cleaner upstream and thus good for drinking

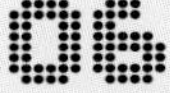

Which of the following statements is wrong about chimpanzees?

A. They are able to acquire human language

B. They can use tools

C. They can walk upright for a short distance

07 **When a male gorilla reaches maturity, the hair on its back will turn _____ in color.**

A. White

B. Silver

C. Gold

08 **What is the main difference between New World monkeys and Old World monkeys?**

A. The former have a flatter and wider nose, with outward-facing nostrils the latter have a narrower nose, with downward-facing nostrils

B. The former have very long tails; the latter have tails

C. The former live in trees; the latter live on the ground

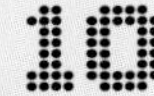

What is the color of a polar bear's skin?

A. Transparent **B.** White **C.** Black

10 **What does a mandrill do when it is threatened?**

A. Screams loudly

B. Bares its canine teeth

C. Climbs up higher

ANSWERS

HERE YOU GO...

01B 02C 03C 04A 05A
06A 07B 08A 09C 10B

PERFECT 10!

I'm not a born genius, it's just that I do a lot of reading in my free time!

SCORED 8 TO 9

To achieve my ambition, I must try harder!

SCORED 6 TO 7

Seeing animals in action in their natural habitat is much more interesting than researching sterile facts!

SCORED 4 TO 5

Sometimes I... find difficult... to speak what... I know, but... I will not give up!

SCORED 2 TO 3

Huh? B-but I love observing animals! This must change!

SCORED 0 TO 1

What?! Jake is smarter than me? No way!